AFTER MIDNIGHT

SHARI NICHOLS

CITY OWL
PRESS

AFTER MIDNIGHT
Raven's Hollow Coven, Book 4

CITY OWL PRESS
www.cityowlpress.com

Cover Design by MiblArt. All stock photos licensed appropriately.

Edited by Heather McCorkle.

For information on subsidiary rights, please contact the publisher at info@cityowlpress.com.

Print Edition ISBN: 978-1-64898-287-3

Digital Edition ISBN: 978-1-64898-288-0

Printed in the United States of America

PRAISE FOR SHARI NICHOLS

"Romance and intrigue collide in Shari Nichols' latest installment of the Raven's Hollow trilogy. Midnight Temptation is a can't-put-down read where the chemistry between Gillian and Garrett pulses with palpable desire, and the twists and turns keep you holding on for dear life. Buckle your seatbelts and enjoy!" - *M. Kate Quinn, Award-Winning Romance Author*

"Her plot was solid, her characters were complex and her writing hooks the reader right from the start and never let's go! Think of a multiple loop, fast, curving, upside down roller coaster and you have an idea of what you are in for with this book." - *Stephenee, Nerd Girl Official*

"Great read and start to a new series. I'm excited to see more of as it comes out!" - *Book Junky Girls*

"I was hooked from page one! A titillating, fast-paced read, this edge-of-your-seat paranormal romance kept me guessing." - *Sky Purrington, Bestselling Author of Time Travel Romance*

"An emotional, action packed, YUMMINESS ride!" - *Carrie Book Fairy*

"I can't wait for what is next in the Ravens Hollow series. I give this book 5 Fangs!" - *Maria Suarez, Paranormal Romance and Authors that Rock.*

"Action packed steamy paranormal romance with a host of intriguing characters." - *Crystal's Many Reviewers*

"The chemistry between the characters is awesome! You won't want this story to end. Looking forward to the next book by Shari Nichols." - *Chris Clemetson, Romance Author*

"I loved the take-charge heroine and the vampires!" - *SFWBC*

"Your path is illuminated by a road-map of stars. I am here to guide you!"
— *Ambika Devi*

"We need not feel ashamed of flirting with the zodiac. The zodiac is well worth flirting with."
— *D. H. Lawrence*

"I will look on the stars and look on thee, and read the page of thy destiny."
— *Letitia Elizabeth Landon*

CHAPTER 1

BROOKE

"*I* don't think I can handle another douchebag today." Brooke Howe cracked a smile as she glanced over at her best friend Arabella. She looked hippy chic in a white tee, ripped jeans, with strings of beads around her neck.

The two had become best friends while living together at a local coven with five other witches. Cutting through the rows of tarot cards, incense, copper bowls, and spell candles, Brooke's heels click-clacked against Enchantment's black and white tile floor.

"When I think about Nico Denopoulos, the words 'gorgeous' and 'hunk' come to mind, definitely not 'douchebag.' Did you forget you're doing a personalized match for him this morning?" Arabella asked, drawing her dark brows together. Reaching for a china mug and a tin of tea leaves off a shelf, she set them up next to the coffee table book she wrote about Tassography.

"Crap, that's today?" Brooke's heart skipped a beat. Nico was the hot younger brother of their friend Willow's husband Alex. They met at their wedding, and like the majority of the females there, she'd been riveted by his black, wavy hair and soulful dark eyes. He epitomized handsome and sexy in one unforgettable package. He'd shown up at the reception with a plus-one, but apparently now he was single and looking to mingle.

Rushing behind the counter to the spot where she kept her calendar, Brooke scanned her matchmaking appointments for June. Nico's name was written in pencil, next to a reminder to get her brows threaded and pay the electric bill. "You're right, as per usual." Having a psychic for a best friend meant it came with the territory. She reached for her still-steaming cup and took a sip from her Matcha latte, burning her tongue.

"What's up with you? You've been in a funk for the past few days." Concern laced Arabella's voice.

"Joe and I broke up. It's the start of a new season, I shouldn't be surprised." At this point Brooke knew the drill. Eventually, malaise would settle in and then she'd shake it off and start over. A deep ache moved through her. She forced a smile. "I'm either an eternal optimist or a sadist. At this point I'm not sure anymore."

"I'm so sorry, Brooke. I didn't know." Arabella walked over and pulled her into a hug.

Brooke eased back and shrugged. "You'd think I'd be used to it by now, but rejection still sucks." *Chalk one up to the curse of the matchmaker.* It was one of the reasons she started her business in the first place: to help others find love, something otherwise elusive to her. She'd been laser-focused on growing her client base by offering extra services like date-coaching and image consulting. Eventually, she wanted to branch out and write an advice column for a magazine.

"It always does." Arabella gave her a sympathetic smile and began rearranging the books on the shelf.

"It's not like I got that fluttery sensation in my stomach when we were together. And the sex wasn't anything special. So why am I feeling this sense of loss?" She'd dated her fair share of zodiac signs, from the crazy Geminis to the unyielding Capricorns, in an attempt to put herself out there in hopes of changing her fate. But every relationship ended the same way.

"You can't give up hope. There are other single guys out there—guys like Nico."

"You're right of course, but I don't know if I can withstand any more heartache. As for Nico, he's strictly off-limits. He's now an unofficial member of our friend group and a potential client."

Brooke had two choices: sit and wallow in self-pity, or seize the cosmic opportunity to help her next client find love and cater to his tastes, however vanilla or kinky. Thinking about Nico and some kind of kink brought a host of sultry images to mind. She redirected her thoughts to doing his birth chart. Once Brooke got that out of the way, then she'd search her database and find three women who would be perfect for him.

At least she could try and look human when he got there. She pulled out her mirror and checked her reflection. Her eyes looked dull, and her cheeks lacked color. Before she could swipe some lip gloss across her lips or add a little blush to her cheeks, the bell dinged, and the door swished open. Smoothing a hand down her black sheath dress, she was glad she wore her old standby. It was laundry day. This had been the only clean thing left in her closet.

Nico Denopoulos strolled into the shop, and just like the last time Brooke saw him, all the air left her lungs in one big rush. She'd seen her fair share of good-looking men, but Nico was in a class of his own, a six-foot-four Greek god, with a chiseled face, sculpted cheekbones, and a powerful build that hit every one of her hot buttons. Black scruff darkened his strong jaw. She could imagine it scraping against her skin in the heat of passion. The caramel color of his skin caught under the glow of the lights. She swallowed hard and tried not to drool.

"It's good to see you again, Brooke." Nico joined her at the counter and pressed a kiss to her cheek. A spark of electricity rippled through her and scattered her nerves. He smelled incredible, masculine and sexy, with a hint of cologne. He pulled back, and his appreciative gaze swept over her face. "You're looking well. I believe the last time we saw each other, there was a whole lot of clapping and cheering going on."

Her cheeks flushed at the memory. "And tequila shots being consumed." He was too much of a gentleman to say he'd caught the garter at the reception, while she'd been the one to catch the bouquet. There'd been an undercurrent of attraction pulsing between them from the moment they met. She'd never forget the hot glide of his fingers or the look of heat and amusement in his eyes when he slid the scrap of lace up her bare thigh. She'd been crawling out of her skin with embarrassment, and she couldn't get over the sensation that she'd known him before.

He smiled wide. "It was a fun wedding."

"Yeah, it was. Why don't we go into my consulting room?" Brooke motioned to the storeroom.

"Lead the way." Dark eyes rimmed with enviable lashes stared back at her. Everything about him was big and masculine, from his hands to his corded forearms. Joe had only been about an inch taller than her, so she'd traded in her heels for flats. She'd always feared he'd drop her on her ass when he tried to carry her, unlike Nico, who looked like he could lift her with one hand.

Nico's heavy footsteps trailed behind her as they crossed to the storeroom. The familiar scents of lavender and rosemary mingled in the air and put her at ease. They stepped through a purple drape into her cubby. "Please, have a seat and make yourself comfortable. I'm sorry it's the size of a matchbook." Arabella had helped her feng shui the small space by painting the walls cream and adding a few of her favorite watercolors. The finishing touch was setting her desk in a commanding position. A small fountain set on the opposite wall, bubbling with a relaxing stream of water. A piece of green jade sat on her desk, next to a cherished photo of her standing beside her brother Drew, right after they'd hiked up Bear Mountain.

"No need to apologize." Nico glanced around the room, nodding his approval. "I like it. You've made great use of the space."

Ignoring the fluttery sensation in her stomach, she smiled at the compliment. She pulled out her phone and turned on her jazz playlist, hoping it would get them both in the zone. "Thanks. Congratulations on your restaurant. I've been planning to stop in for dinner, but I heard it's hard to get a reservation." Nico looked like a giant standing in her tiny room. His blue cotton shirt stretched over his broad shoulders and what looked like slabs of hard muscle beneath.

"You don't need a reservation. You're welcome any time." His gaze slid to hers and got her warm all over. She'd never been so aware of a man in her life. He emanated a hot, sexual energy.

"I appreciate that," she said with a nod. "How did you come up with the name 'Gemini' for your restaurant? Tell the truth, are you a closet astrology buff?" she teased, hoping to calm the butterflies floating around in her stomach.

A deep chuckle rumbled from his chest. He sat down in the chair across from her and stretched out. When his leg brushed against her thigh, awareness prickled along her skin. Her physical reaction to him unnerved her. She ignored the sensation and leaned back in her desk chair. "No, not at all. My partner thought it sounded cool. It's strictly a coincidence."

"Trust me, there are no coincidences." This morning when Brooke checked her horoscope, it said she'd cross paths with someone that would change the course of her life forever. Did Nico have anything to do with the ominous prediction?

"Ah, a matchmaker who believes in fate."

If he only knew the half of it. "I admit, I'm one big cliché. But it's my truth." Nico didn't strike her as the type who'd have any trouble finding a date. Charisma rolled off his broad shoulders in waves. "Well then, if you're ready, we can get started. May I ask why you're interested in using a matchmaker?" Without thinking, she reached up and toyed with the blue topaz on the chain around her neck. The stone had been a gift from her dad and Drew for her twenty-fifth birthday.

"This was Willow's idea," he pointed out. "She raved about your matchmaking skills. When your sister in-law gives you a suggestion, you take it, even if magic and witchcraft aren't my thing." In the enclosed space, she caught another whiff of Nico's cologne and could smell summer on his skin.

Focusing on the man in front of her—and not the sexual fog flitting around in her brain— she tilted her head to the side. "Don't worry. This isn't about me putting a spell on you or another person, or making you drink a potion to fall in love. It's about using astrology to match you up with the perfect person for you, and to see if your stars align."

He leaned back in his chair and visibly relaxed. "It seems all the women I'm interested in already have boyfriends or are seeing someone. I guess my timing has been off."

The story of my life. "It's always about the timing. You can think of what I do as bringing the human element to getting matched. Do you mind if I ask about any previous long-term relationships, and what your current dating habits are like?" The second she posed the question, a flair of disappointment welled in her chest. While a part of her was still sad over her breakup with Joe, she couldn't stop imagining herself on a date with Nico. Shaking her head, she refused to go there.

"I don't have a lot of time to meet people. And when I do go out, I don't have much in common with the women I meet online. Their priorities are different. They're always looking over their shoulders for the next best-thing. The truth is I'm tired of swiping right." Nico ran a hand through his hair. His raw honesty softened her heart.

"Fair enough. I'm guessing you and your date from the wedding broke up?"

"The sparks just weren't there. I value family and my job keeps me pretty busy, so I want to share my off time with someone who's worth it, someone who's exciting. I want to explore the world with that person." His gaze locked with hers and the air shifted between them.

"Hmm, I think I can help. I appreciate your honesty and trusting me with your love life." Damn that sounded corny. "I assure you everything's strictly confidential. Okay, are you ready to get started?"

"You've certainly piqued my interest. How do you match me up?" His gaze narrowed as he glanced over at her computer.

"I use a combination of astrology, algorithms, and my Ephemeris." Brooke pointed to the leather-bound tome on her desk. "This book gives me insight as to what the solar system is doing, the planets' positions, retrogrades, eclipses, and, well, the signs from above."

"It's like your Escoffier, the main book we chefs use to learn how to cook."

"Exactly. Good analogy. I take your personality traits and goals, and then I match you up with someone who has similar ideals. These women will be vetted and background checked, as well as checked out on social media. Why don't you tell me what you're looking for?" she asked, holding her breath, waiting for his reply.

"I'm looking for my soulmate."

Brooke almost fell off her chair. How refreshing. "Wow, most of my clients don't speak in such honest terms." She didn't know guys like him even existed. His romantic heart spoke to her on every level, another reason to avoid gorgeous, charismatic men like Nico Denopoulos at all costs. Even if she was interested, things wouldn't work out. They never did.

A smile flashed across his handsome face. "I like to be upfront. So what's the first step?"

"I can do a personalized compatibility report to help you find your matches and get you started."

"Willow says you've got a gift for matching people up." A spark of excitement flared in his eyes.

"Thanks." She swiveled in her chair, angling her head to a collage of photos of some of her clients on the opposite wall. "We've seen seven marriages and seventeen engagements."

"I'm in your capable hands." A shiver moved through her at his intimate tone. An image of Nico in all his male glory flashed through her mind. From the size of his hands and feet, she'd bet her Ephemeris he'd be well-hung. She turned back to face him, trying to keep her expression neutral.

"Are you okay?" His gaze traveled the length of her, making her whole body tingle. "You're all flushed."

Busted. "Uh, this room tends to get warm." She cleared her throat and turned the fan on high. "If you decide to move forward, you'll be matched with three dates per week, for three months."

"And you personally choose them?"

"I hand pick every single one. I'll be matching you with women you're astrologically compatible with. We can discuss things like generosity, values, humor, chemistry, and hobbies beforehand. You can contact me anytime, day or night." She handed him her card with her cell number on the back. "I'm extremely dedicated to all of my clients." Why did her voice sound throaty on the last part?

Nico flashed a sexy smile that would make any of his dates lose their minds—and their panties. "I appreciate that."

"I typically start out by asking some questions and then doing a complimentary birth chart." She motioned to her screen. "It's based on the astronomical snapshot of where the stars and constellations were the moment you were born."

"Willow said you might ask me that question, so I called my mom."

From the sweet way Nico said her name, Brooke sensed their closeness and found the connection endearing. "Awesome. You came prepared."

"I was born March 21, 1996. At 2:00 p.m."

"An Aries." Brooke would've guessed it anyway. A fellow fire sign, Aries men were passionate and confident, with fiery personalities. They were known for their strong bodies, commanding presence, and dominating sex appeal. But Nico was on another level. She'd leave out the part about them being romantically and sexually compatible. She'd never been attracted to her astrological equivalent before, but none of those men had been as charming as Nico.

Humor lit his eyes. "So what you're telling me is that it's okay to ask a woman her sign?"

She laughed. "Well, yes and no. How about we leave that part to me for the time being?" Brooke picked up the astrological wheel on her desk and pointed to the center. "These wedges are the houses. Each one represents a different aspect of our lives. The creative house is what propels you cook up those culinary masterpieces I've been hearing about at your restaurant."

When he smiled, his eyes crinkled at the corners. "To be determined after you've sampled my food."

Brooke refrained from asking if that was a personal invitation and pointed to the pie-like sections of the chart. "The seventh and eighth houses are the most important, in my opinion. They're the houses of love, partnership, marriage, and sexual relationships. I'll be using them as indicators to find your soulmate."

His gaze narrowed. "You really take this stuff seriously."

"I do," she said with an audible sigh. "Our astrological charts hold the key to everything in the universe."

"I know a heavenly body when I see one." He winked and pointed to the circular sphere on her desk. "I'm referring to the stars and planets, of course."

"Of course." And the man could flirt.

When swallowed, his Adam's apple bobbed up and down in his throat. Strength and virility practically oozed from his pores. "What about fate? Do you believe some things happen for a reason?" The direct way he asked the question made her think of lazy days in bed and hot, sweaty sex.

"Absolutely." She tried to get her thoughts in check and stared at her screen. After she input his birthdate, a set of designed questions popped up. "Time for a quiz. I'll match you with the sign that you're best suited with romantically based on your score. How would your friends describe you? Passionate, smart, talented, cool, funny...?"

"Passionate." Every time Brooke looked over at Nico her heart raced.

"What about hobbies? Besides your exuberance for cooking?" She pounded away on her keyboard, focusing her attention on creating his profile.

"I enjoy watching football with the guys, going to sporting events, and running down by the river when I have the time."

"Those are all great." She added his responses to his profile then looked up. "What makes you mad?"

The humor drained from his eyes, and she sensed she'd hit a nerve. "Liars."

"Noted. Your sun sign can vibe with certain colors. What's your personal favorite?"

"Purple."

Brooke could guess his answer to the next question. "Which of these dates would you prefer the most? A fancy restaurant? Going for a hike? Talking under the stars? Parachuting? Or chilling on the couch and binge-watching your favorite show?"

A genuine smile spread across his handsome face. "Talking under the stars would be at the top of my list."

Mine too. She needed to stay in business mode and not get swept up by the hunger in his eyes when he looked at her. What was the point? Like all the others, he'd forget about her when the season changed. The fallout could put a strain on their friend group "What does love mean to you? A strong physical connection or a strong emotional one?" The question sent a flush of heat to her cheeks.

His gaze burned into hers as he leaned closer, forcing an involuntary rush of breath from her lips. "If you don't have physical attraction then there's nowhere to go, but there has to be a strong emotional connection, or you burn out fast."

"I agree." Her cheeks burned with heat from the intense look in his eyes. "There's another matter we should get out of the way. I strongly urge my clients not to engage in sex unless there's monogamy. Rule number one in the matchmaker's handbook."

He chuckled. "The matchmaker's handbook?"

"You can think of the book as guidelines that I strongly urge my clients to follow. What are your thoughts about kissing on the first date?" *Why the hell did I include that one?*

His gaze moved from her face to her lips. "I say yes, if we're both into each other and the moment presents itself."

His words made the room seem too small, and him too close. Those damn butterflies took wings and fluttered around in her stomach. "Let's move onto compatibility and intimacy. I'm going to recommend people who you're destined to click with, and let the universe pick your matches with a little help from me."

Amusement flashed in his eyes. "I'm game on everything except for your no-sex rule. Can we negotiate?"

A shiver moved through her at his words. "What did you have in mind?"

CHAPTER 2

NICO

The smell of Brooke's perfume filled Nico's head and made him want to groan. "If this astrology stuff works, can I delete my dating apps?" he asked, leaning back in his chair, trying to relax. Being this close to Brooke had him flustered. *Does she have any idea I've been secretly fantasizing about her for months?*

Brooke rested one slender hand on the leather book on her desk, a look of certainty flashing in her eyes. "All you need to do is lean into the process and leave the rest to me. My engagement and marriage numbers go up every day because astrology works."

Nico smiled at the pride in her voice. Talk about taking a leap of faith. As Brooke typed on her keyboard, his gaze slid to her profile. She wore her blonde hair twisted up in a bun, with loose pieces falling over the slim column of her neck. His gaze moved lower to her pink dress. The color brought out the blue in her eyes, and the fabric dipped low in the front, showing a hint of cleavage. Long, toned legs peaked out from under the desk and sent his pulse jackhammering. He could barely string words together the first time they had met at Alex and Willow's rehearsal dinner.

He'd been drawn in by her whimsical air. But after spending some time talking to her, he found her to be sweet, and self-deprecating, with a great laugh. He wanted to ask her out right then and there, but he heard she was seeing someone. He just hoped whoever he was, he treated her right. "This system has been used for centuries to connect couples and help them find love and fulfill their desires," Brooke's sultry voice interrupted his thoughts.

My desire's sitting right in front of me. "So what you're telling me is that my sun sign determines who I'll be the most sexually compatible with?"

She exhaled a shaky breath. "In a nutshell...yes. Think of this as the science of destiny for those looking for a deeper, more cosmic connection." He found the hitch in her voice mesmerizing.

Their gazes locked, and lit off a firestorm in his chest. He wanted her more than ever. Too bad she was already taken. He'd watched as a steady stream of guys from the wedding took turns hitting on her, not that he could blame them. Her body could stop traffic, and her smile exuded confidence. She seemed to have no idea of her allure, which made her even more attractive.

Glancing at her desk, a vase containing a single red rose caught his eye. He wondered if her boyfriend had given it to her. "How did you get into astrology?"

Darkness stole over her face, extinguishing the lightness in her eyes. "I inherited my gift from my mom, who inherited it from my grandmother." The question seemed to bother her like a secret she kept buried deep. He wanted to ask why, but he didn't want to put her on the spot.

She reached over and handed him a small book, titled *The Zodiac.* "Here, this will give you a quick overview of astrology. Why don't you take a look through this while I finish your chart?"

"Sure." He caught another whiff of her perfume, and his groin tightened against the front panel of his jeans. He wanted to lick her neck and taste the sweetness of her skin. Flipping through the pages of the book, he tried to tamp down his arousal.

Nico imagined doing things with Brooke he hadn't done with any other woman. Sex with her would be exhilarating and passionate. He'd bet they could steam up the sheets and rip them to shreds for days on end.

She'd captured his imagination with her fascination with the planets and stars. By the end of the wedding weekend, Nico wanted her with an intensity he'd never experienced before in his life. And no matter how many times he tried to push her out of his mind, thoughts of her came creeping back, always lurking in the background.

He had enjoyed his fair share of flings, but always became disappointed when they ended. Deep down, he wanted someone to share his life with for the long haul. Could he trust her to help him find happiness? His gut told him she was the real deal. Shaking off his lust-fueled thoughts, he tried to understand the differences between an aspect and a house as he flipped through the pages of the book. Crushing on her would only muddy the waters.

"All done," she said, exhaling a breath and looking up from her screen. "I also offer free couple's counseling once you sign up. I highly recommend a coaching meeting after your dates. Do you have any questions?"

"Yeah, how does astrology determine sexual chemistry?"

The pulse pounded at her throat, and a lovely blush spread across her pale skin. She folded her hands on her lap. "I...um, outline a physical aesthetic that you might find attractive for your ideal partner. I should probably ask what things turn you on."

"Long, deep kisses that last for hours. A partner who's funny and adventurous in bed, and not afraid to ask for what she wants."

Her pupils dilated at the same time her chest rose and fell. Maybe this attraction wasn't one-sided after all. Her hands shook as she resumed typing on her keyboard. "I appreciate your honesty and I'm sure your dates will find your answers extremely interesting."

"What now?"

"I think I have everything I need, except for some photos of you. Once I put the finishing touches on your birth chart, I'll email you a copy, along with the contract, and a link with my fee." She smiled. "No pressure. Read it over first and if you decide you want to move forward, I'll get started on matching you up and helping you fall in love."

Irritation coursed through his veins. She seemed to have no trouble fixing him up with other women. What was he thinking flirting with her while she was trying to set him up? *Way to go.*

Nico surged to his feet before he made a bigger fool out of himself. "Thanks for everything, Brooke. I appreciate your help." He pulled out his card from his wallet and placed it on her desk. "I'll be in touch."

CHAPTER 3

BROOKE

*B*rooke spent the rest of the day doing readings for her clients and scheduling appointments, but she couldn't stop thinking about Nico. Her mouth watered every time she thought about him and his turn-ons, which were now downloaded into her memory, along with his profile.

Once she finished his birth chart, she emailed it to him, along with a short overview of what it all meant with an option for him to call or do a facetime with her to get a more detailed explanation. She purposefully left out the part about the South Node on his chart showing a past life.

Her phone buzzed with a text. She lifted it off her desk and looked at the screen. It was from Nico. She'd put his digits into her contacts just in case.

> Nico: I've attached the signed contract, along with your fee. You're hired, matchmaker.

> Brooke: Thanks. I'll get started ASAP. :)

A few minutes later, her phone buzzed with another text. Three photos of Nico appeared on her screen, each one more gorgeous than the next. Brooke set her phone down on the counter, and sighed. When she thought about Nico going out on dates with other women, her chest grew tight with jealousy. Who was she kidding? Things between her and Nico would never work out, for the same reasons none of her relationships lasted for more than a couple of months. Blowing out a frustrated breath, she spread out her pendulum grid board and her lunar calendar and got to work. By the end of the day, she'd found him three matches, all professional, attractive women.

After Brooke sent his information, including his photos, to all three women, they responded within the hour. *No surprise.* She stared at one of the photos of him at his restaurant and smiled. The image managed to capture the sexy glint in his eyes, but still didn't do him justice. Now all she could do was sit back and allow fate to intervene.

Let the hunt begin.

Five days later, Brooke went around the shop with the candle snuffer, extinguishing every flame. From the moment she'd set Nico's matches in motion, she'd been a walking disaster. Yesterday she'd knocked over an expensive copper bowl, and today she'd whacked a full tray of potions off the counter. She'd started a draft of her book at least a dozen times, but ended up staring at the screen, typing the same sentence over and over again. One of her clients called to report a nasty breakup, and all of her appointments seemed to blend together. She chalked it up to sleep deprivation.

Last night she woke up drenched in sweat and gripping the sheets, on the verge of an intense orgasm. Now the vestiges of her smoldering dream still clung to her and set her off-kilter throughout the day. Nico's lips trailing over her skin…his fingers digging into her hips. A deep male voice whispered her name while he slid in and out of her. She knew the voice.

It belonged to Nico.

Now she wondered why in the world she agreed to fix him up with three other women when deep-down she wanted him for herself. The main reason—things with Nico would never work out. A two-hundred-year-old generational curse that had been passed on to her made sure of it. Images of him laughing and talking to his dates filtered through her head in rapid succession. Breathing in and out, she forced herself to release the white-hot streak of jealousy surging through her veins.

Being a hopeless romantic had always been her big flaw. Growing up, she needed an escape from her parents' constant bickering, so she'd stay up late binge-watching rom-coms until her eyes bled.

Arabella walked up to the counter and clicked a button on the wall, turning the shop's neon "open" sign to off. "Do you want to grab some dinner at Grand Vin? All the ladies are meeting there."

"I'd love to, but I'm exhausted. All I want to do is head home and soak in a hot bath with a glass of wine." She'd become friends with these fun, adventurous women through her cousin Gillian. Now they all shared the profits and the pitfalls of owning a small business.

"If you say so. You've been moping around here for days, and I sense it has nothing to do with Joe and everything to do with Nico." Arabella gave her a sidelong glance. "Why not put us both out of our misery by giving him a call and seeing how his dates went?"

Setting the snuffer down, Brooke rested her hands on her hips. "Wow, am I that obvious?"

"Do you really want me to answer that question?" Arabella collected the empty potion bottles on the counter and placed them in the sink.

Being best friends with a psychic did have its downside, like never being able to keep a secret. "Why do you always have to be right?"

Arabella turned around and fluttered her lashes. "What can I say, it's a gift."

A smile tugged at Brooke's lips. "Maybe I should wait until tomorrow to call. It's after hours, but then again Nico doesn't work nine-to-five. I usually touch base with my clients after a few days." So why did Nico make her hesitate?

In Brooke's experience, Aries men fell in love fast and dove into relationships headfirst. What if Nico told her he was smitten with one of the women she'd matched him up with? It would mean that she'd done her job well. She dug her phone out of her pocket and dialed his number.

"Brooke?" The deep timbre of Nico's voice filled her ears and sent her heart thumping in her chest.

"Hey, Nico, I wanted to check in and find out how your dates went." She held her breath, waiting for his reply.

"I've been meaning to call. You beat me to the chase. My last date just ended, and I was about to head out. I'm still at the W hotel," he said over the noise in the background. "Why don't you meet me for a drink, and I can give you a play by play?"

"A drink?" She hesitated for a moment. *This is a business meeting,* she reminded herself. Why did her voice sound so eager? The thought of seeing him again made her pulse skyrocket. She wanted him to find the love he deserved. She was being selfish. All three women were perfect for him, astrologically speaking anyway.

"I hope your boyfriend won't mind."

"My boyfriend? I don't have a boyfriend."

"Son of a bitch," he muttered. "You're kidding me, but Alex said—"

"We broke up recently. I haven't spread the news." Brooke didn't want to read too much into Nico's reaction, but she couldn't ignore the pang in her chest.

"I could come pick you up and we could go somewhere else." *Why does this sound an awful lot like a date?*

"No, it's okay. I'll grab an Uber and head over as soon as I'm finished here at the shop. See you soon." Brooke's heart fluttered with excitement. She glanced at Arabella. "I guess you heard everything."

"Oh, I heard, and I could smell your pheromones from over here." Arabella chuckled. "It sounds like Nico's interested in more than your star savvy. Go. I'll lock up."

"Thanks, you're the best." Brooke reached for her purse off the counter. "I've got a feeling this night is about to get a whole lot more interesting."

Brooke couldn't remember much about the short drive over to the hotel; her mind was too preoccupied with thoughts of Nico. After she pushed through the revolving doors, she darted through the crowd. Her heels scraped against the parquet floor, mirroring the pounding of her heart.

Perspiration broke out along her neck. She breathed in and out, trying to rein in the butterflies floating around in her stomach. As she approached the bar, she spotted Nico right away. He towered over everyone else and looked mouth-watering in his light blue button down and dark jeans.

Their gazes locked from across the room, and for a moment, she forgot to breathe. Nico exuded an intense masculinity and a natural sensuality that made her heart pound. She'd been drawn to his magnetic presence from the first moment she'd laid eyes on him, and now the sensation only seemed to intensify.

Two-hundred-plus pounds of muscle walked over to where she stood and sent female heads turning in every direction. "You made it."

"I'm sorry. I hope you weren't waiting long." Brooke caught a whiff of his sandalwood cologne, and fought the urge to sigh.

His searing gaze trailed over her face and then slowly down her body. "It was worth it." He bent his head and kissed her cheek. The press of his lips on her skin made her tingle. She'd never been this attracted to another person. "Thanks for coming," he said close to her ear as they walked to the bar.

"Of course."

"What would you like to drink?" Nico pushed the barstool out for her with a smile.

Hopping onto the stool, Brooke set her clutch on the bar. "I'll have white wine. I can't wait to hear about your dates."

His poker face gave nothing away. "Well, my first date with Claire started out okay. We talked for a bit and got as far as the appetizer when she started asking what I was doing for Thanksgiving. After she gave me her timeline for getting engaged and having kids, I decided we weren't a match and ended the night early."

"Oh, no. She came across so normal in her interview, maybe a bit type A." She shook her head. "I feel terrible."

"Don't. It's not your fault. These things happen." He signaled to the bartender.

The bartender came back and set a goblet in front of her on a cocktail napkin. "For the lady."

"Thank you." She pulled out her wallet.

Nico's hand closed over hers and sent a jolt of electricity zinging up her arm. "This is on me."

She glanced down at his long, tapered fingers covered with tiny red marks and found the fact that he worked with his hands as sexy as the rest of him. "Okay, but the next one's on me. Back to your dates, what about Emily? The teacher? She's a Sagittarius. You're a perfect match. Did you two vibe at all?" she asked, taking a sip of her wine.

"She's a nice woman, but there was zero chemistry. It felt like I was on a date with my sister, and I don't have a sister. Besides, she's still hung up on her ex, so I gave her some advice." Nico angled his barstool to face her and folded his arms across his wide chest.

"You gave her dating advice? Whoa, it sounds like I might have some competition. Do tell. What did you suggest?"

Nico laughed, and the sound tightened her chest. "I told her to call him."

"From your date?"

A spark of mischief flashed in his dark eyes. "Yeah, they talked and then she left to meet him. Who knows, maybe they'll invite me to their wedding."

Her heart melted. Talk about being a good sport about the whole thing. And of course, it only magnified his hotness. "I checked her out beforehand and she said she was single. I'm so sorry."

"Hey, it's okay." Nico squeezed her knee, sending a rush of heat between her thighs. "I don't doubt you."

"What about your third date with Lydia? The attorney?"

Nico frowned. "She treated the wait staff like crap and sent her food back twice. I told her I owned a restaurant, but that didn't seem to deter her behavior. In fact, it got progressively worse throughout dinner."

"Nothing like this has ever happened before." *Could fate be playing her hand?* "I'll refund your fee back in full, Nico."

Heat smoldered in his eyes. "I'm not disappointed at all. I don't know if I believe in the stars aligning or in some cosmic force, but I can't help but think that this all happened for a reason—maybe because we're both single at the same time."

Warmth radiated from her chest. The tension twisted her stomach into another knot. It would be so easy to get caught up in the idea of being with Nico. But the inevitable fallout would be devastating within their friend group. Nico, I..."

"Do you remember when you asked me what my favorite color was?"

The vibration of his voice made her ache all over. She nodded and gulped her wine, catching a slight buzz. "Aries typically favor red."

"But I chose purple for the color of the dress you wore at the wedding."

A surge of heat spread from her cheeks to her neck. His sweet words blew through the last of her defenses. "You remember the color of my dress?"

"I remember a lot of things, tiny details about people that interest me." Their gazes locked, and she couldn't look away from the heat and hunger burning in his eyes.

"I...didn't know. You never said anything." Brooke stared at his lips as he lifted his glass. They were full and sensual, perfect for kissing.

"I heard you were taken, and I didn't want to be a jerk." The deep timber of his voice slid into her blood, igniting her desire.

"I was, but we broke up." When the season changed, so did his feelings. And like all the others, she never heard from him again. *Another ghost situation.* She wondered why she even bothered to date anymore, but then loneliness would creep in through the cracks of her heart, and she'd dive in again.

"I'm sorry, but the way I see it, this is my lucky day. The truth is I've been thinking about you for months now."

The admission sent her heart galloping. His charisma made him shine brighter than any star in the sky. *Why get excited?* They'd go out a few times, have some fun. And based on the chemistry pulsing between them, they'd have mind-blowing sex that would last for days. But then summer would turn to fall, and he'd forget all about her, and she'd be left broken-hearted.

"Seeing you again brought my attraction back full force. Keep your fee, Brooke, and go out with me."

A thrilling sensation moved through her, but she ignored it and pushed on. "I'm flattered, believe me, but I can't. I don't date my clients. It's a strict rule of mine."

"Technically, I was only a client for about five minutes." His phone beeped. He glanced at the screen and muttered a curse. "I'm sorry. I have to go put some fires out at the restaurant." Nico pulled out his wallet and slapped some cash on the bar. "Let me drop you off and make sure you get home safely."

"I appreciate it, but it's out of your way. I'll be fine." She didn't want to be alone with him in a confined space. It would be too tempting.

Nico looked like he wanted to argue, but eventually shook his head. "Let's get out of here." He rested his warm hand at the small of her back as they walked to the front doors. Searing heat singed through the thin material of her dress, and she swore her panties caught fire.

They stopped at the revolving double door as well-dressed couples walked in and out of the hotel. He leaned down and kissed her cheek, and a soft hum of electricity sparked between them.

"Think about what I said. I'm not going anywhere, unless I read the situation wrong, and you're not interested."

"No...it's not that. Quite the contrary, but I hope you understand why I can't go out with you. It may sound silly, but I have rules about these types of things."

"I respect your decision, but I want you to remember one thing." He bent his head and whispered close to her ear. "Rules are meant to be broken."

Her breath lodged in her throat. His words left her flushed and too aware of every scorching inch of him. She watched as he pushed through the doors onto the sidewalk and disappeared through the crowd.

Sighing with arousal and frustration, tonight she'd nix the bath in favor of an ice-cold shower.

Brooke stood at the greenhouse stove helping their potions guru, Saje, heat up a batch of concoctions for the upcoming Founder's Festival.

"How did it go with Nico?" Her cousin Gillian stood at one of the butcher block tables piling crystals, sticks of incense, and candles into a box. "Arabella filled me in." The curse only affected those on her maternal line, so thankfully her cousin was spared.

A flush spread to Brooke's cheeks. "As it turns out I was zero for three on the matches. But we talked, and it was amazing. He ended up asking me out."

Saje looked up. "Wait, I'm confused. You agreed to fix him up with other women, even though you've been infatuated with him for months?" She moved to one of the other tables covered in splotches of candle wax. Her dark ponytail swung back and forth as she filled a mortar and pestle with lavender and wormwood and ground them into a fine dust.

Releasing a long, deep breath, Brooke filled them in on the finer points of the evening. "So you see why I can't go out with Nico?"

"There's a reason none of Nico's dates worked out. He's supposed to be with you." Gillian added a pile of their business cards, brochures, and handmade lotions to the box and then sealed it up. "Why not give him a chance? He's a great guy, and he's seriously fine."

"Agreed. He's also charismatic and easy to talk to." The more time Brooke spent around him, the more she swore they'd known each other in a past life. She sighed deep. "The fact that he's sexy as sin doesn't hurt. And we're compatible, astrologically speaking. I checked with my pocket Ephemeris and our stars align."

Saje wiped her hands on her apron. "Even more reason to go out and have some fun. Sometimes you need to trust your instincts and go with what feels right."

"I get what you're saying, and I hate to sound like a Debbie Downer, but things won't work out. They never do. It's time I accepted my fate." Turning off the burner on the stove, Brooke forced a smile. She'd pored over every spell and incantation she could find on lifting the curse, but nothing ever seemed to work. "Why would things be different with Nico?"

Placing the box aside, Gillian walked up next to Brooke and rested a hand on her shoulder. "Maybe nothing's worked because you haven't found your true love. What if Nico's 'the one?'"

A flicker of hope blossomed in Brooke's chest and then burned out like a candle flame. Could she dare to dream of something real and long-lasting with Nico? An ache welled inside her. How much more could her heart take before it shriveled up and grew as cold as ice? "Maybe I do need this." *Am I taking a chance at love or setting myself up for more heartache?*

CHAPTER 4

NICO

*N*ico couldn't remember the last time he'd been this nervous. Drawing in a ragged breath, he walked up the torch-lit path that led to the sprawling Victorian mansion, hoping he didn't overdo it with the aftershave. He still couldn't believe Brooke had agreed to go out with him on a real date.

The lights from inside the manor glowed like a beacon in the night. Lifting the brass cauldron knocker, he banged it against the old wooden door. He tapped his foot to release some of the adrenaline coursing through his veins. None of the women he'd dated made his pulse throb or his mouth go bone-dry like Brooke did.

The door opened, and Brooke appeared in the doorway, her form silhouetted under the lights. His breath caught. She wore a fire-engine red dress that hugged her body and showed off her curves. "You look beautiful." When he leaned in and kissed her cheek, her sweet scent filled his head, and a yearning stirred inside him. She smelled good enough to eat.

"Thanks. And you look very handsome tonight. Come in. I'll just grab my purse."

He stepped inside and drank her in. Blonde hair brushed past her shoulders in soft waves. His hands clenched at his sides with the urge to run his fingers though the silky strands and find out if they felt as soft as they looked.

"Where are we going?" she asked, turning back to face him, excitement sparking in her eyes.

"It's a surprise."

"Oh? I'm not big on surprises." She held up her hand. "I'm sorry. I know that sounds weird."

"No, not weird, but maybe cautious. Are you used to being in control of everything?" He'd love to find out why. The craziest thing was he wanted to know everything about her, good and bad.

"Not everything," she corrected and gave him a sultry smile that made his heart pound.

Pulling a scarf out of his pocket, he held it up. "May I put this blindfold over your eyes?"

Brooke busted up laughing. Not the reaction he expected. The warm, feminine sound swept some of his nerves away. "Whoa, five minutes into our date and you're already pulling out a blindfold? You didn't mention you had a kinky side." The air hummed with sexual energy.

"You didn't ask." He winked and caught the flare of surprise in her eyes. "I was going for spontaneous, but I'll go with kinky."

Her cheeks turned a lovely shade of pink. "I guess I'm being a hypocrite. I recommend spontaneous adventures to my clients all the time."

"Maybe you need to start taking your own advice." Nico brushed the back of his fingers over her face. "You're blushing."

"Nico...I...Please, proceed."

"Trust me," he whispered and came up behind her, and all couldn't stop thinking about her naked in his arms. His erection pressed against the front panel of his dress slacks. He secured the blindfold over her eyes and then tied the end into a knot. "No peeking."

"Wow, you're really taking this seriously."

"You'll see why soon." Nico wanted to let her in more than any woman he'd ever met, which was crazy. They barely knew each other. He reached for her hand and laced their fingers together, loving the way they fit. They walked out the door and stepped into the sultry night air. "Careful, watch your step." He pulled her close as he led her to his car.

"No hints?" she asked from beside him.

"Patience." He opened the passenger door and helped her inside. He admired her willingness to go along, even though she'd been pushed out of her comfort zone. After he got into the driver's side, he started the car and cranked the AC. The July heat permeated through the windshield and made the seats hot.

"I think I have a nickname for you." Brooke fumbled around in the dark and pulled her seat belt across her shoulder.

Nico arched his brows. "Yeah? Let's hear it."

"TDM—tall, dark, and mysterious."

"As far as nicknames go, that one's not half bad. Now I'll have to come up with one for you." He shifted the car into gear and pulled into the flow of Saturday night traffic.

Her head whipped back against the seat rest. "Whoa, I can tell this is a fast car."

He glanced at her as she crossed and uncrossed her smooth, shapely legs, and stifled a groan. "It's a Mustang. She's my pride and joy." He gripped the wheel and focused on keeping his eyes on the road.

"I keep learning something new about you."

"You already know a lot about me. I want to learn about you. How long have you lived in Raven's Hollow?"

"All my life. The Howe's were some of the first founders of the town. What about you?"

"Our family has roots here as well. My great, great-grandfather came here from the island of Crete and opened the first tavern in town."

"How interesting. And now you're picking up where he left off with Gemini?"

"I guess so. I moved to LA for a stretch and tried to open a restaurant out there, but things didn't work out." That was an understatement. "I moved back a few years ago to be near my family. Do you have siblings?"

"I have a younger brother I'm super close to. Sadly, he moved to Atlanta recently." They slowed for a light, and she turned to face him, pushing her hair behind her ear. "How far are we going? Should I have packed a bag? Or a passport?"

"You don't need any of those, but I may have forgotten to tell you to bring a helmet."

Brooke laughed. "Hmm, what would require a helmet?" She pressed her finger to her lips. "Bungee jumping? Snowboarding? Mountain biking? I don't think I'm dressed for any of those."

"Good guesses, but you forgot skydiving and hang gliding." Nico grinned, enjoying their playful banter. He turned onto Grand Street and pulled into Gemini's empty lot. "We're here." He'd closed the restaurant for their date and paid the staff to take the night off. His partner wasn't exactly thrilled with the idea, but he understood. He'd never done something this insane in his life. But Brooke was worth the effort.

"Okay, but just so we're clear, it's not a dungeon somewhere I'll never be heard from again, right?"

"Close, it's my basement where I keep all my sex slaves." A vivid image of Brooke naked and tied to his bed floated through his head. He was glad she couldn't see his face or the bulge in his pants right now, or he'd be in big trouble. "Maybe you're not used to being on the receiving end of things."

Her sharp intake of breath told him she might've been imagining the double entendre. Now all he could think about was licking her while she exploded in his mouth. He'd bet she'd taste every bit as good as she looked.

Opening her door, he led her inside by the elbow. "I'm looking forward to having you all to myself." After he pulled out his keys, he unlocked the door and ushered her inside. "Watch your step. Hold my arm. I won't let you fall."

"It smells amazing in here."

"Almost as good as you." He pulled out his phone and clicked on his playlist. The soft notes of a saxophone filled the dining room. "Don't take the blindfold off yet."

"We're at Gemini, aren't we? Is this the surprise?"

"Welcome to my second home. We're closed for the night, so we have the whole place to ourselves."

"I can't believe you brought me to your restaurant and closed the whole place for me." Nico picked up on the awe in her voice, solidifying his decision. "I don't know what to say."

"You said you've been meaning to stop by. I figured I'd give you the best seat in the house." Nico eased her down in a chair at a white-clothed table, laden with roses and candles for the occasion.

"This is by far the most romantic thing anyone has ever done for me." Romantic gestures would be routine if he had anything to say about it.

"I think it's your turn for a quiz. I'm going to make you use your senses. What do you smell?"

She inhaled, and a smile broke out across her beautiful face. "Rosemary, basil, and garlic."

"Good girl. Let's see how you do when it comes to your sense of taste. Here goes." Nico lifted a cracker and cheese from a tray and held it to her pretty, pink lips. "Open up."

She sniffed the cheese, and took a bite. "Yum. I love the tangy flavor. Pecorino cheese?"

"I chose my personal favorite. Are you ready for another bite?"

"Yes." Her little pink tongue darted out to wet her lips. "What's next? Don't tease me."

"I think I'm going to enjoy teasing you." He picked up a sautéed mushroom. "Open wide."

Her lips closed over the mushroom. "I taste the rosemary; it's so good." Her soft groan of pleasure sent his imagination into overdrive. If he could give what they were doing a name, he'd call it food porn.

"I think it's time to wash the food down with something to drink." Nico picked up the wine opener and got to work. The pop of the cork echoed through the dining room. After he poured some wine into a glass, he set the bottle on the table. He lifted the glass and swirled the Cab around to let it breathe. "Are you ready?"

"Go for it."

Tilting the glass to her parted lips, he loved the sexy way she swallowed and worked her throat. "Mmm, Cabernet?"

"Right on the money. A lady that likes good food and wine. Do you want to take the blindfold off?"

"Keep going. I'm enjoying myself." Nico wanted to lick the wine from her lips, taste the sweetness of her mouth.

Lifting a rose out of the vase, he brushed the petals over the side of her jaw, earning him a delicious shiver. Then he held the rose under her nose. "This one can't be eaten."

A deep inhale followed by a smile. "Roses, my favorite. How did you know?"

"I noticed you had one in your office the other day."

"You must've been paying attention."

If she only knew how much, he might scare her away. "I think it's time to take off the blindfold." He set the rose back in the vase. "I want to look into your eyes."

Brooke reached up, undid the scarf, and pulled it off her face. She gasped as she glanced around the room. "I can't believe you went to all this trouble for me."

"It was no trouble. I prepared everything ahead of time. I loved doing it. You have a crumb there." Nico wiped it from the corner of her mouth and put it to his lips. Awareness hummed between them.

She took a sip from her goblet. "I'm psyched to try your food. Tell me the story behind this place?"

"It has been a lot of hard work," he said, refilling their glasses. "Backbreaking sixteen-hour days, but it's all starting to pay off. I never thought I'd get to this point. This has always been my dream." Nico left out the part about almost losing everything and angled his head to the kitchen door. "I hope you're hungry."

"Starving."

Nico wanted passion in his life with someone he could see himself with for the long haul. The rush of excitement pumping through his blood got him thinking that someone could be Brooke.

CHAPTER 5

BROOKE

*B*rooke gazed at the real china on the table and the bouquet of red roses in the vase, and she shook her head, dazzled by the lengths Nico had gone to for her. Candlelight flickered in the dark room, adding to the romantic ambiance.

"This is beautiful, Nico." Heated glances and lingering smiles replaced any shred of first date awkwardness. The idea of spending time alone with him left her breathless with anticipation.

"I take it you're not used to being spoiled." Nico picked up a mushroom from a fancy white plate in the center of the table and popped it into his mouth. He looked mouthwatering in a short-sleeved black dress shirt that clung to his arms and broad shoulders.

"Put it this way, my last boyfriend wasn't big on romance. Give him a drive-up window and a six pack, and he was good to go."

His shoulders shook with laughter. The sexy rumble turned her insides warm. "That's awful and, frankly, surprising as hell."

"I know what you must be thinking, if I'm a matchmaker, why in the world would I settle?" Sipping her wine, Brooke looked at him over the rim of her glass.

"I admit the thought crossed my mind. You deserve flowers and candles, every night of the week." *How can he be real?* Nico sounded too good to be true.

"I want to believe in the fairy tale. So you kiss a few frogs while searching for your prince," she said over the strum of guitar music playing in the background, hoping that didn't sound pathetic.

"I hope you find him." His gaze sent heat unfurling inside her. Nico reached across the table and squeezed her hand. His touch made her shiver. "Let's eat. I'm ravenous all of a sudden." He got to his feet and pushed in his chair. "Do you cook at the manor?"

"No. But the other girls do, and I buy groceries, so it works out well."

His mouth twitched in amusement. "I can teach you. Are you ready for a tour?"

"I can't wait." Brooke followed him into the kitchen. The scrape of her heels against the tiled floor echoed through the large space.

"Watch your step over the mats." Nico motioned around the kitchen. "This is the line where all the magic happens."

Everywhere Brooke looked gleamed silver. She went behind the counter, where stacks of white plates, condiments, pots, pans, and knives of every shape and size were stacked on big, silver racks.

"I'm just going to heat up our tortellini. I made the pesto earlier." Nico went over to a giant walk-in fridge, pulled out a few containers, and a wedge of cheese. Then poured oil in the pan and turned on the flame.

"I'm impressed with what you've accomplished," Brooke said, motioning around the kitchen." "You've gone after your dream and made it a reality."

"It took me a while, but here I am. What about you? Tell me about this boyfriend you just broke up with, or is it a sore subject? I'm sorry if I'm being intrusive. I want to get to know you better." Oil snapped and sizzled in the pan.

"No, it's okay." Like all the others, it was a short relationship, the story of her dating life. "We weren't meant to be, but I suppose he was nice enough."

"Nice?" He drew his brows together. "That sounds pretty lame."

"What's wrong with nice?" She watched Nico as he lifted the pan and tossed the tortellini like only a chef could. Sweat broke out along her forehead and slid down her neck from the heat radiating off the grill.

"You strike me as a woman who wouldn't settle for nice." His hungry gaze raked over her and left her hot and needy. "The words passionate, exciting, and spontaneous come to mind."

His keen observation left her breathless. Nico pointed out everything she ever wanted or needed but could never ask for because it would only lead to heartache. Brooke pushed her niggling doubts aside and focused on staying in the moment.

"Now it's your turn." He motioned for her to join him at the burner. "Give it a try. It's all in the wrist."

"I tend to be a klutz in the kitchen. I hope you have an extinguisher nearby in case I set anything on fire."

He laughed. "I'll be right here."

"Here goes." Wrapping her hands around the handle of the pan, she tried to mimic the same motion she watched Nico do, but she didn't come close. "You make it look so easy."

"Let me help you." Nico came up behind her and lifted her hands, and she became aware of every hard inch of him. His warm breath fanned her neck, leaving a trail of goose bumps along her skin. "Back and forth, slow and easy. Yeah, that's it." The smell of his cologne and his deep voice in her ear made her shiver. Talk about sensual overload.

"I never knew cooking could be this fun." Brooke sucked in a breath, so turned on she could barely breathe. She'd be whipping up a meal every night of the week if she had Nico in her kitchen.

"You smell better than anything I'm cooking."

The impulse to lean back into the solid wall of his chest and bask in the strength and comfort of his arms took hold. The pull between them was scorching hot. She knew, deep down, in the pit of her soul, that they'd be magical together.

"All finished." After Nico spooned the tortellini and the pesto onto their plates, he grated cheese over the top. He picked up their plates, and they headed to their table.

When they sat back down, Brooke set her napkin on her lap. "This looks amazing." She didn't waste any time digging into her pasta. The creaminess of the pesto and the basil hit her taste buds right away. "This is delicious. You're spoiling me."

A wicked smile played across his lips. "Get used to it. Your eyes flutter when you're enjoying your food. I can't help but wonder when else you do it."

Her fork clattered onto her plate and the air became thick with sexual tension. "Do you always say what's on your mind?" She gazed at him across the table, cataloging the details of his chiseled face. She didn't think she'd ever get tired of looking at him.

"I'm sorry. I didn't mean to offend you." Taking a bite of tortellini, he chewed and swallowed, then took a long pull from his wine glass. "I don't like to beat around the bush. How did you get into matchmaking?"

"I majored in psychology in college and studied sex and relationships. I'd been doing readings for my friends and got the wild idea to combine the two," she said, wiping her mouth with her napkin, grateful for the change of subject.

"It makes sense."

"Seeing other people find love satisfies me." Brooke couldn't tell him that a two-hundred-year-old curse hung over her head like a noose, dooming all of her relationships to end when the season changed.

Nico nodded and listened with rapt attention. "I don't doubt you're good at what you do. Although the jury's still out on the women you tried to fix me up with," he said in a playful tone. "I think what you do is sexy."

Every cell and nerve ending tingled with their growing connection. When it became too much, Brooke turned away. She glanced around the dining room at the crystal chandelier hanging from the coffered ceiling and the upholstered benches built into the wall. Everything about the décor epitomized casual elegance. "This place is incredible. I'm so happy for you. How did you do this all on your own?"

"I have investors and a partner, my best friend from culinary school. We're looking to expand eventually."

"It doesn't surprise me after doing your chart. You have Jupiter in your eleventh house, which rules your goals, and aspirations. I admire you for what you've accomplished. It's not easy to open a small business."

"I can be stubborn when I want something." Heat smoldered in his dark eyes. "What about you? What are your dreams, Brooke?"

Her finger traced the stem of her wine glass as she considered the question. "I want to grow my business. I've always dreamed about having an advice column about dating. I've submitted some blog posts to a few different magazines. I haven't heard back, but I'm not giving up. I started a book about astrology. Who knows, maybe I'll get around to finishing it one of these days."

"You can do anything you want to."

His words made her warm all over. She loved his enthusiasm. After that, they talked nonstop about their favorite books and movies, and places they'd like to visit. The conversation flowed and, once again, Brooke got the feeling that they'd known each other in another lifetime.

"Nico," she whispered, loving the way his name rolled off her tongue. "What does your name mean?"

"People of victory. It's of Greek origin. It got me into trouble growing up with two older brothers because I wanted to be the boss, but my mom always came through for me."

Her heart turned over when she tried to imagine Nico as a little boy with his coal black eyes and mop of dark hair. "Are you two close?"

Closing his fingers together, he nodded. "We're like this." She picked up on the affection in his voice.

"How nice for you." She wondered what it must've been like to grow up with a family like Nico's. They finished their pasta and pushed their plates aside. "I'm stuffed. You're the one to blame if I bust out of this dress."

"Feel free to take it off at any time," he said in a husky voice. "There's still dessert."

"How many women have you swept off their feet with this grand gesture?" Brooke motioned around the room with her hand. This blew all of her first-date suggestions out of the water.

"You'd be the first, Miss Howe." The admission washed over her and made her giddy.

"You make me feel special, Nico."

"You are special." He reached for her hand. His thumb caressed her fingers, sending delicious sparks along her skin. The air turned thicker, heavier.

"You've got this lust for life…this Aries allure that's hard to resist."

"I get this is a first date and I don't want you to think I'm coming on too strong, but I feel this connection to you like no one ever before." He shook his head. "It's kind of scary."

Her breath hitched. "Yeah, I know what you mean."

"I have a serious question." His dark eyes flashed with sexual promise.

Her other hand gripped the side of her chair to steady herself from the ache between her thighs. "Go ahead."

"Do you like chocolate cake?"

Exhaling a breath, she smiled. "It's my downfall."

"Then get ready to go to the dark side."

Twenty minutes later, they shared a decadent slice of molten lava cake with a peanut butter filling.

Afterward, she leaned back in her chair and rubbed her belly. "I'm ready to explode."

"I know a great way to burn up some calories." Awareness prickled up her spine. Nico got to his feet and came over to her side of the table. "I thought we could dance."

Her heart skipped a beat. "Oh."

"Why don't you take off your shoes? Your feet must be killing you in those heels. I'm not complaining." His gaze roamed over her legs and made her shiver.

Before she could respond, he got to his knees and slipped one of her sling-backs off her foot. Warm fingers massaged her arch and her heel. Her head fell back on a moan.

"When you make that breathy sigh, I can't help but imagine you aroused." The heat radiating from his voice took her breath away.

Her belly clenched against the sudden heat pooling there. His words forced her to press her thighs together. All night long she'd been thinking about ripping his clothes off and jumping his bones. "Nico…"

"Feet are erogenous zones." The way he kneaded with such skill and care left her hot and needy. Who knew a foot massage could get her so turned on? Apparently, he did. He took off the other shoe and paid the same attention to her other foot, heightening her attraction for him to a painful degree. He stood, held out his hand, and helped her to feet.

Craning her neck, she gazed up into his dark eyes. "I think you have the height advantage."

"Step onto my shoes." Nico took her hand in one of his and rested the other at the small of her back. They moved to the music like they'd been dancing together for years. He pulled her close, and she became languid in his arms.

"Where did you learn how to dance?"

"I took lessons once upon a time." A shadow passed over his face. She wanted to ask what had put it there but decided against it for now. "I've been waiting all night to hold you in my arms." The rhythm of their breaths mingled together.

She got the sensation of falling even though he held her tight. "This night has been magical."

"For me, too." Nico lifted her chin up with his thumb and gazed at her lips. Hunger burned in his eyes. "I can think of a few ways it can get a whole lot better. I've been dying to kiss you all night." He bent his head and his lips brushed against hers, sweet and tentative at first. But when he sucked on her lower lip, she moaned and opened for him. His tongue swept into her mouth in deep, velvet strokes, scorching her clean. He tasted like wine and chocolate, sweet and decadent.

His fingers moved to her back and brushed across her skin in the most sensual way. She dug her fingers into the lush strands of his hair as the kiss raged on. Tilting his head to the side, he deepened the kiss, making her toes curl. The lush sweeps of his tongue forced her to draw breath. Her breasts ached and grew tender. Her clit throbbed, along with her heart.

A low primal groan escaped from his lips, and she didn't think she'd ever heard anything sexier in her life. The drugging taste of his mouth stirred her hunger. She could see herself becoming an addict, always looking for the next fix. She'd always dreamed of a lover kissing her like this, making her burn.

His erection pressed against her stomach, hard and incessant. Nico pulled away and fastened his lips to her neck. He trailed open-mouthed kisses along her collar bone. "I want you, Brooke, so damn much it hurts. I have from the first second I laid eyes on you. I've been fantasizing about you for months, but I was conflicted because I was with someone else. It also made me realize that she wasn't the one."

Her chest heaved. "I want you too, Nico, but this is all happening so fast." She didn't jump into bed on the first date, but his sultry kisses fired something wild and wanton in her blood.

"This isn't like me." He pressed his forehead to hers. "Getting to know you has only made me want you more."

Her knees weakened. Desire thrummed between her legs. She'd never experienced this kind of frenzied passion before.

"All I could think about while I was making tonight's dessert was licking the chocolate off your bare skin."

Her nipples tightened from his words. What could she say to that?

"Come home with me, Brooke," he rasped, pressing another sensual kiss to her lips. "I know we should wait, and that I should woo you properly. If we have sex too soon it might start this relationship off in the wrong direction, but all I can think about is being inside you."

Her heart banged away in her chest. "Nico…I…"

"I want to make you come, Brooke. You have no idea how much. It's driving me insane."

Nico's raw, honest words made her ache and aroused her even more. A voice in her head told her to cut bait and call it a night, but another voice told her she might not ever get this chance again. She preached romance and spontaneity to her clients all the time, so why shouldn't she experience it for herself? Placing her hand on his chest, she found his heart pounded in the same wild rhythm as hers. "How long does it take to get to your place?"

Scorching heat flared in his eyes as Nico's hand moved to her ass and squeezed. "We can be there in fifteen minutes if I speed."

A rush of desire flowed through every cell and nerve ending. Why should she deny herself a hot night of passion? Their need for each other melted the last of her defenses away. "What are we waiting for?"

CHAPTER 6

NICO

*B*y the time they made it to Nico's apartment, he was crawling out of his skin. He unlocked the door, pushed it open, and then reached for Brooke in the dark. This time when his lips found hers, there was nothing sweet or gentle about the kiss. Their breath mingled, and their teeth collided. His mind hazed with desire. Heat rushed through his veins like hot lava.

He registered her kicking off her shoes, his lips never leaving hers as he lifted her off her feet. Her legs wrapped around his waist as he walked through the hall to his bedroom on shaking legs.

Though he'd been with his share of women, he'd never experienced this kind of intense passion before. He laid her down on the bed and flicked on a light. "Tell me if I'm going too fast."

"Don't stop," she whispered.

Moonlight streamed into his room and caught in her hair, the blonde strands now fanned out on his pillow. Her lips were red and swollen from his kisses. He couldn't remember ever being this hard before. From their first conversation, he'd wanted this woman. *I need to calm the fuck down and make this last...make this good for her.*

"What are you thinking?"

Swallowing the lump in his throat, he stared at her face. "You're beautiful." Her long fingers brushed over the bulge in his pants.

"So are you. I can't believe you're real."

"I'm going to take this slow and drive you out of your mind." He gave her another deep kiss and crawled over her on the bed. Their bellies brushed, and slow, dark heat flared once more.

"I'm already halfway there." Her head fell back in a moan, revealing the slim column of her neck. Ducking his head, he placed a kiss there, and the flowery scent of her perfume filled his head, rocking his world.

Fumbling with the side zipper on her dress, he slid the fabric down her body. When he caught a glimpse of her black lace bra and matching thong, a hot rush of blood shot straight to his groin. "Jesus, Brooke. Are you trying to kill me?"

Instead of answering him with words, she pulled his mouth down for another wet kiss.

Nico broke away and bent his head to suck on her nipple through the lace. "I can smell you. My cock has been hard from the first moment I saw you in that dress. You have no idea what I've been thinking about doing to you all night." *Why hold back now?*

"You're making me crazy." Brooke reached out and cupped him through his dress slacks.

He bit back a curse as her slender fingers rubbed back and forth. Every time he looked at her, his chest swelled. She was different from any woman he'd ever met; her sweetness shined through from her soul.

Desire flared in her big blue eyes. "Nico," she murmured on a breath filled with need.

"I've got you, Matchmaker."

His heart pounded clear up to his throat as he reached down and unhooked her bra. Small round breasts fell into his hands. Groaning, he pulled one rosy tipped bud into his mouth.

Brooke arched into him, murmuring incoherent words of pleasure as he sucked and licked. She was so willing and warm—so responsive and sexy.

His thumb circled over her nipple, earning him a shiver. Moving to her waist, he caressed her soft skin and then squeezed the curve of her hip, wanting to learn every inch of her luscious body. He stopped at her inner thigh. His fingers brushed over the seam of her thong, and she gripped the sheet, moaning low in her throat.

Gritting his teeth, he pushed the silk aside and touched her folds for the first time. *Damn.* His mind hazed with need when he found her soaking wet and swollen. He inserted a finger and rubbed her clit back and forth, over and over again, until she writhed beneath him.

"Nico...I need..." she breathed.

"I know what you need. I want to drive you to the edge, torture you slowly. You're so fucking hot." As he slipped her thong down her body, her legs fell open on a sigh. His mouth gaped, staring at all her pretty, pink flesh. "You're beautiful here too." He resumed teasing her clit in deep, long strokes, using his thumb to drive her wild.

Her moans grew louder. Her chest heaved, and she squeezed her eyes shut. "I'm going to come."

"That's it, baby. Come for me." Watching Brooke come apart might be the hottest thing he'd ever seen.

She clenched around his fingers, scalding him with her liquid heat. Nico kissed her long and deep, swallowing her cries of pleasure. He never wanted this to end, and he knew, with every fiber of his being, that this was only the beginning.

Brooke

Panting hard and almost feverish from a mind-blowing orgasm, Brooke tried to catch her breath. "What you're doing feels so good."

Warm fingers roamed over her ribcage and down her hips, leaving a trail of heat and raw need in their wake. His hands moved across her belly. "Your skin is like silk. I could touch you all night. I'm not finished with you yet," he murmured in a voice thick with lust. And then his dark head moved down her body.

"How could you wrench any more pleasure from me?" They barely knew each other, and yet there was this familiarity when he touched her that forced her shyness away. She lay before him stark naked while he remained fully clothed.

"I want to try. I've been dreaming of ways to get you off." He lifted his head. The way he looked at her like she was all he could see made her wet and throbbing for his touch and his mouth.

Gripping the sheets, she held on for dear life as his tongue slid into her belly button. He moved lower, to her inner thigh, and her hunger built again.

When he lifted her leg and licked her behind the knee, she nearly jolted off the bed. "This is sensitive."

His mouth moved to her core, sending a flush of perspiration along her skin. The first sweep of his tongue made her gasp. He licked and sucked on the sensitive bundle of nerves, adding a finger, coaxing every last drop of pleasure from her body.

Another orgasm rolled through her in a slow, heated wave of pleasure, but Nico didn't let up for a second. He continued to lick her while curling a finger inside her, stroking back and forth. Ecstasy rippled through her, scorching every nerve ending. Her response to him was almost embarrassing. Searing heat sizzled through her veins like fire as another orgasm crashed over her and made her gasp.

She laid there feeling boneless, trying to catch her breath. "Your turn." She pushed up to her knees, eyeing the thick ridge of Nico's erection through his dress pants. Excitement built low in her belly as she reached for his belt buckle. "Why are your clothes still on?"

"I can remedy that right now. I can't wait to be inside you." He shook off his pants and kicked them to the side, revealing muscular thighs.

Her fingers shook as she helped him unbutton his dress shirt and tugged it off his broad shoulders. She tried not to gasp at the deep ridges of hard muscle contouring his chest, abs, and that sexy "V" at his pelvis. The man put Adonis to shame. Her lips parted in wonder. "How do you look like this? How often do you go to the gym? There's not an ounce of fat on you."

"It's all I have time to do these days when I'm not working. I've had a lot of pent-up sexual energy these past few months, and all because of a certain matchmaker."

Her hand stilled as she looked up into his face. "So you really were attracted to me all this time?"

"From the first moment we met." He cupped her cheek and caressed her chin. His heated gaze swept over her, and the truth of his words reflected in his eyes.

"I was wildly attracted to you too. I even had this dream about you." Brooke skimmed her fingers over his chest, loving the way his muscles bunched beneath her fingertips. She stared, transfixed, taking in every slab of honed muscle.

His gaze darkened and turned smoky. "I can't wait to hear all about it. Maybe we can act it out the next time."

Before Brooke could wonder if there'd be a next time, Nico slid his boxers down and his magnificent cock jutted out. Her mouth watered at the sight of him in the flesh. He was thick and long with a heavy crown. She couldn't stop staring. She swallowed and tried not to drool. She gripped him in her hand and rubbed back and forth. He was rock hard and smooth, like silk over steel.

"You don't know how many times I've thought about you touching me. Too many to count." Nico grew heavy in her hands. His head fell back. A primal sound escaped from deep in his throat. His jaw tightened. "You need to stop, Brooke. I can't hold on."

As soon as she released him, he moved to open a drawer and pulled out a condom from the nightstand. She heard foil rip open, and then he sheathed up his cock.

They reached for each other at the same time, tumbling sideways onto the mattress. Her head pressed into the pillow, her anticipation building and cresting. She parted her legs to accommodate him. "Nico, I need you."

"I'm right here." He gave her a sexy smile. "We have all night." Climbing on top of her, his weight dipped the mattress. The tip of his erection poised against her dripping center. "You're so wet for me." He slid in a little, enough to let her adjust to his size. He remained braced above her as sweat beaded on his forehead. "Are you okay?"

"Yes, please," she begged.

He eased in a little more, and then in one deep thrust, he became seated to the hilt. His growl vibrated through her, tightening her core. "You feel so good. You're so tight."

She cried out as his cock slid in and out of her, deep and intense. A shiver moved through her limbs and left her shaking. She gasped at the sensation of him filling her, making her burn. Pulling out and kissing her again, his tongue tangled with hers, stealing her breath. When he slid back in, he moved in and out until they found their rhythm. He pounded harder and faster, sending her to the brink of another orgasm.

"Fuck, Brooke—"

Her skin tingled. She'd never been this hot before. She needed him closer, deeper. She couldn't get enough. She dug her fingers into his back, her nails running down his skin, hoping she didn't draw blood, relishing every deep thrust. Everything about him turned her on.

He kissed her neck. "I love hearing the sexy sounds you make when you're mindless with pleasure. I want to hear you say my name when you come this time."

The frenzy of his passion ignited another rush of heat. Her core clenched around his cock as flames of heat licked against her skin. Pleasure rippled through her limbs, hot and greedy as another orgasm raced through her bones. "Nico…"

"Come for me again, Brooke." His voice sounded rough. Not letting up for a second, he lifted her bottom and plunged deeper, hitting her from another angle.

She moaned and turned her head away, barely able to keep up with the sensations taking hold of her. It was too much.

"Look at me." He cupped her chin and forced her gaze to his. A mixture of lust and warmth flared in his eyes.

He lifted her hands above her head, and laced their fingers together, like he wanted to be one with her body as well as her heart. He pumped faster and groaned while he whispered sweet, erotic words in her ear. The passion in his eyes and his voice captured her in its claws. His weight pressed her into the mattress.

The way he moved his hips made him go deeper. He hit her core over and over again. Panting, he stroked his cock in the same spot while she quivered beneath him. "I can't hold on," he ground out the words. His pace quickened as he plunged deeper. "Are you close?"

"Yes…I'm coming." Another orgasm raced over her, filling her vision with light and color.

His whole body shook as he came, long and hard. He collapsed on top of her while she tried to catch her breath. The sounds of their hearts hammering away echoed in the small room. He scooted up and kissed her eyelids and her nose. Then he placed a kiss on her lips and looked down at her with awe. "Holy shit, Brooke. That was out of this world."

Her entire body still pulsed and tingled from the aftershocks of multiple orgasms. He'd given her the hottest sex of her life. She'd read the Kama Sutra and recommended the book to her clients. She gave them advice about love and intimacy, but nothing in the world could've prepared her for sex with Nico. Had he ruined her for all other men?

"I'll be right back. Don't move." Placing a kiss on her lips, he got up and removed the condom, tying the end, and throwing it in the trash. He walked to the bathroom, giving her a great view of his ass.

"That's easy, I can't." She stretched her arms over her head and smiled. Her limbs felt like jelly. The scent of sex and Nico's spicy aftershave lingered in the air.

"Now there's a sight I could get used to, you naked in my bed." He emerged from the bathroom buck naked, holding a towel, then climbed back into bed.

Shutting off the light, he wrapped her in his arms, and pulled the comforter over them. She listened to his heartbeat slow down as he drifted off to sleep.

She'd never experienced this all-consuming passion before. And she sensed deep down that Nico might be the only man on the planet who could give it to her.

CHAPTER 7

BROOKE

*S*unlight streamed in from a crack in the vertical blinds. The sounds of traffic and car horns forced Brooke awake. She glanced around Nico's small bedroom and found her dress and undergarments folded on a desk chair. Tingles from last night still clung to her skin. Sultry images rushed through her head in rapid succession, each one more vivid than the next.

Strong arms wrapped around her in a tight embrace. Nico's warm breath fanned her neck, and her heart squeezed. She could get used to waking up like this. She wanted to stay here all morning in this cocoon. But she couldn't because whatever they started wouldn't last.

In the light of day, her head spun. She'd broken every one of her own rules. She'd slept with Nico on the first date. Granted, the sex had been out of this world. But it was so unlike her to get down and dirty this fast. She craved order, and right now, everything felt out of control.

She'd lectured all of her clients about the dangers of leading with sex. She drummed it into their heads for a reason. Oxytocin and endorphins get released, which leads to intimacy, a sense of false expectations, and disappointment in big fat spades. *Shit, shit, shit.*

Self-preservation kicked in and jolted her out of her sex-muddled brain.

"I need to get out of here," she muttered and untangled herself from Nico's strong arms.

Glancing at him over her shoulder, he turned onto his back, and threw his arm over his head. Delicious scruff darkened his cheeks and jaw. She sighed deep, taking in his thick lashes and messy hair. If only she could stay here and make love to him again, wake him up in the most sensual way. He'd already ruined her for all other men by being sweet, romantic, and scorching-hot in bed.

How bad would it hurt when he forgot all about her? At least this time she'd be the one to end things before she let them go any further. After she reached for her bra, she slipped it on and then stepped into her dress, sans underwear.

Before she could contemplate the situation any further, she grabbed her heels and her purse, wishing she didn't have to do the walk of shame out of his building. She prayed she didn't bump into anyone she knew, especially a client.

Pulling out her cell, she ordered an Uber. She grabbed one of her cards and a pen to leave a note. She turned it over and wrote the first thing that came to mind.

Thx for last night. It was fun. B.

How lame. She inwardly cringed. She set the card on the pillow and pushed a stray hair off Nico's forehead. Her chest tightened as she stared at his sleeping form, committing every gorgeous detail to memory.

A wave of sadness washed over her as she tiptoed out of the bedroom and walked out the door. Deep down, she knew it was for the best.

"Hold on. Let me get this straight. Nico closed his restaurant for you on a Saturday night, cooked you dinner, got you roses, and gave you multiple orgasms?" Gillian stood behind the register, closing it out for the day. She looked up and stared at Brooke like she'd grown another head. "And you just left without saying goodbye?"

Fortunately, the shop was empty, or their customers would've gotten an earful. Brooke grabbed the keys off the hook and began locking the crystal cases. They decided to close early for a coven meeting back at the manor to discuss preparation for the upcoming Founder's Festival.

"Yup, I'd say that about sums it up. The more entangled I get, the worse it will be when he leaves me." Brooke needed to protect her heart, but at what cost? She hadn't stopped to consider Nico's feelings in all this. "What I did was selfish. I instantly regretted leaving the moment I walked out the door."

"I can only imagine the sex being combustible from the way you two looked at each other," Saje chimed in, walking through the store picking up empty Dixie cups that had been filled with their daily potion. "You're going to end things before you even give Nico a chance?"

Ignoring his calls and texts had been a shitty thing to do. Guilt sat in her stomach like a brick. She'd call him eventually and apologize when the heat between them died down. Then she thought about what she'd say when she did call. Something along the lines of, "I'm a coward," or "I've been cursed," didn't seem apropos. Every time she thought about him, sensual images flooded her mind. She'd never been experimental in bed, but he made her want to try everything by being a generous, passionate, hot-blooded lover. He'd given her the best sex of her life. "Nico will move on." And she'd be left broken hearted.

"You don't know that for sure." Gillian stacked up her tarot decks and tied them in a ribbon. For all her cousin's headstrong ways, the Taurus in her wanted the best for Brooke.

"My seventh house has always been a complete shitshow. The curse has made sure of it. Let it be for now, Gillie, please." Brooke tried to ignore the way her stomach twisted. She hated how she'd left things with Nico. She exhaled and picked up her phone off the counter, checking her calendar for her upcoming appointments, trying to stay busy.

Saje walked up to the counter and set down the tray of potion cups. "I've been doing some research and I may have come across a potion with an accompanying spell that we haven't tried before."

"I appreciate all you've done, Saje, believe me, but I don't know if I have it in me to keep doing this." How many more times could Brooke get her hopes up only to have them shattered again? "I don't think I can take any more heartache."

Gillian came up and pulled her into a hug. "You've got to believe things will change. If Saje could concoct a potion that managed to turn Garrett from a vampire into a human again, then anything's possible." Gillian and Garrett shared true love, full of mess and emotion, ups and downs, but they somehow endured.

Tears misted in Brooke's eyes as she pulled back. What would it be like to dream about someday with a guy like Nico? "Good point. I'm sorry, I don't know why I'm being so emotional."

"There's no need to apologize." Gillian squeezed her arm.

"Thanks, for always being there for me. I want you to know how much I appreciate the love and support." Exhaling a breath, she pointed to the flier on the counter. "Have we come up with a theme yet for the Founder's Day Festival?" Brooke asked, eager to change the subject.

"What if everyone dresses up as their favorite witch and wizard?" Gillian tilted her head to the side and her light brown ponytail fell over her shoulder. "You could ask Nico to go as your date."

Shaking her head, Brooke smiled at her cousin. Gillian could be as persistent as a bad rash. But she did have a point. Nico would make the night memorable. Everyone in their friend group was blissfully happy and in love. Alex and Willow had been the first couple to tie the knot. Garrett and Gillian were next. A couple of months back, Alex's special agent partner, Cayden, had surprised their friend Natalya with a romantic proposal. As for Saje, she was in love and living with her hunky demon boyfriend, Nick. And Brooke remained in the same place. Alone. "Who knows, maybe I can get a few more cats."

"I can already feel a sneeze coming on." Gillian clicked the neon "open" sign off.

The bell dinged and the door opened and closed, blowing in a light summer breeze. "Nico?" Brooke sensed his magnetic presence right away. The scent of his cologne filled the shop. She spun around and her breath lodged in her throat. "What are you doing here?" The sight of him made her ache.

His thick brows knitted together. Anger and confusion flared in his eyes. "Can we talk?" He looked as gorgeous as ever in a green Gemini T-shirt, faded jeans, and damp hair. "I hope I'm not interrupting anything," he said, glancing over at Saje and Gillian, who seemed to be listening to every word.

Gillian came up and gave him a hug, breaking the tension in the air. "No, not at all. We're just about to close."

And before Brooke could stop them, both women grabbed their things and headed for the door. The two waved good night.

"See you in the morning," Brooke mumbled, shutting the door behind them. After she slid the lock in place, she turned back to face Nico, hoping he couldn't hear the wild thump of her heart.

"I want to know why you took off this morning without waking me up and saying goodbye." Hurt laced his voice. Nico's chest expanded on a deep breath as he took a step closer.

"I'm sorry, Nico. There's no excuse for what I did, but I don't have sex on the first date. I broke rule number one in the matchmaker's handbook."

"We're back to that? There are no rules when it comes to this kind of thing." His voice softened, charging the air between them.

"I freaked out. My flight instincts kicked in. I was wrong." Brooke sighed. "You didn't deserve it, especially after going out of your way to make the night special and romantic, but I figured it was better to rip the Band-Aid off clean. It makes things less awkward for everyone."

Anger flickered in his eyes. "I guess you made the decision for both of us then? What if I told you that this wasn't a one-night stand for me? You would've known that if we talked."

Setting the keys on the counter, she blew out a breath, mentally kicking herself for offending him. "True. I shouldn't have left. I'm really sorry."

"Apology accepted. I was hoping to wake up to a warm, sleepy woman in my arms, and not a cold bed." Nico took another step, closing the distance between them. His proximity muddled her brain.

He'd somehow managed to obliterate all of her memories of sex with any other guy in one incredible night. "Why don't we go to my office and talk?" Since she'd never stopped to think how this might affect him, she owed him that much.

"I'm right behind you." He followed her to the back. This time when they got to the purple drape, he pushed it aside and motioned for her to go ahead of him into her office. He took a seat in the chair next to her desk and she sat across from him on a cushioned stool.

Heat smoldered in his eyes. "I could smell you when I woke up. I can still taste you on my lips."

His words made her flush. "Nico." Her nipples hardened, beading against the silk of her blouse. All day long she'd thought about the strength of his arms, pulling her closer, his hips arching to push deeper inside her. The slow, sudden ache between her thighs became uncomfortable.

"What are you thinking about, Brooke?" he asked in a low, intimate tone that reminded her of their naked bodies tangled together. "You're red all over."

She cleared her throat. "Things moved fast. I'm not used to getting my head caught in the clouds." She'd never experienced this connection to another person before. And she didn't know how to navigate the situation.

"I understand better than you think." His words shredded the barrier she tried to maintain. He ran a hand through his damp hair, making it stand on end. "I haven't been completely honest with you. I should've told you right from the start…"

Her stomach knotted. "Told me what?"

"I'm divorced."

The words hit her like a poison dipped arrow to the heart, which was ridiculous and made absolutely no sense. But then the thought of Nico still having feelings for his ex-wife coated her throat like acid. *I'm being a hypocrite.* "You never said anything when I asked you about your longest relationship." Brooke tried to keep the accusation out of her voice and failed. She had zero claims on him at this point.

"You're right and I'm sorry for omitting the truth and not being upfront from the beginning." A wave of tumultuous emotions swirled in his eyes.

Her thoughts spun in a million different directions, and one thing became clear, Nico had the power to hurt her like no other man. "You don't owe me anything."

"I think I do. Please, let me explain."

CHAPTER 8

NICO

*L*eaning back in his chair, Nico hated the look of betrayal flaring in Brooke's eyes. He wanted to give her time and space, but her taste and touch beckoned him here. Now seeing her in the flesh ignited a raw passion inside him that he couldn't ignore. She was so pretty it almost hurt. He damned himself for his weakness and hoped like hell he could make things right.

"The reason I didn't tell you from the get-go was because I was embarrassed."

"Why? There's nothing to be embarrassed about. We all have pasts. I'd never judge you." Her gaze narrowed with concern. "Why don't you start from the beginning?"

Now he'd have to reveal the whole sordid tale and hope like hell she'd look at him the same way. "I was twenty-two and fresh out of culinary school. I worked my whole life and saved up some money. I moved to L.A. with big dreams." He sucked in a breath and the smell of candles and incense flared in his nostrils, along with the flowery scent of Brooke's perfume.

"You planned to open your first restaurant there?"

He nodded. "I worked as a Sous Chef at one of the best restaurants in the city, with the goal of making a name for myself."

"Is that where you met your ex-wife? In L.A.?" The soft lilt of her voice gave him the courage to continue.

"She worked as a waitress there and things got serious pretty fast." He heard her sharp intake of breath, which made him happy in a selfish way. At least he knew she cared on some level. He'd never been the jealous type, but the thought of Brooke with some other guy got his blood boiling.

"Why did you get a divorce?"

"It turns out my ex was only interested in my money, not that I had a lot." His pride still suffered the hit. He fought the urge to push the memories back to the hole from where they came. But Brooke deserved to know the truth.

"Nico, that's terrible." She leaned forward and reached out to squeeze his hand. "What happened?"

"My ex drained everything. When I asked her about money missing from our account, she'd find a way to manipulate the conversation and make me feel guilty for working all the time. The more I worked, the more she'd spend."

A line formed between her brows. "I can't imagine how hard that must've been for you." Her voice hitched with emotion, anchoring him to the present.

"By the time I realized what was happening, it was too late." He ran a hand over his face. "One day I came home, and she was gone. And so was the last of my bank account."

Her gaze lit with compassion. "I'm so sorry you went through something so awful. Most people would've given up. How did you pick yourself up and start over?"

The question washed over him, flooding his mind with painful memories. "I came back home with my tail between my legs and worked my ass off. Things get put into perspective after you lose everything. I found some investors and never looked back."

The warm, reassuring smile playing across her lips reminded him of her sweet, caring nature. She couldn't be more opposite from his ex. "You're a survivor, Nico. You created your own success, despite a terrible experience, because you're strong and excellent at what you do."

Her compliments made his chest swell with pride. "The whole thing screwed my head up for a while. It's the main reason I haven't gotten serious with a woman." But Brooke made him want to try.

"I'm not surprised after everything you've been through. And yet you were willing to take another chance on love. What brought back your faith in humanity and allowed you to trust again?" she asked in a tentative voice.

"All this time I thought I was getting something over on my ex by being bitter and lonely. But then I realized I was taking poison and expecting her to die. I couldn't give her that power over me anymore."

"I admire how you didn't let a bad experience make you jaded." She smiled. "I have no doubt that you'd rise from the ashes. You have an Aries moon."

He chuckled and placed a kiss on her knuckles. "Do you believe everything is tied into the stars?"

"Well…yeah, it happens to be a system backed up by thousands of years of research and study." Her words ignited his affection and passion. "I think it helps to make sense of the world around us."

When he looked into her eyes, he expected to see pity or judgment, but only sincere empathy shined back at him. "So, you see, I don't take this kind of thing lightly." He let go of her hand and reached over to brush his thumb across her cheek. "All I could think about when I woke up and you weren't there was this sense of loss. There was this intensity to our love making that I've never experienced before. I can't explain it. I know it makes no sense."

"I get it…believe me, but there's something about me you should know." He caught the alarm in her voice. "It might change your mind about us."

"Trust me, that's not going to happen." He placed a finger to her lips. "You don't need to tell me right now. I think there's been enough soul-baring for one night, don't you?"

"Yeah, I suppose you're right." She exhaled a long, deep breath, looking relieved.

"You'll tell me when you're ready." Scooting his chair closer, he leaned over and pressed a kiss on her cheek. "See, I know you better than you think."

"Oh?" Her nose wrinkled in the most adorable way.

"I know you're sweet." He kissed her temple, breathing her in. "I know your eyes roll back in your head when you eat chocolate lava cake." His cock strained against the front panel of his jeans. "I know you make these little breathy sounds when you're about to come..."

"Nico." She tilted her head back, giving him access to the slim column of her neck.

"I know you like to be kissed right here." He nipped her behind the ear, earning him a shiver.

"I don't have any willpower against you," she whispered on a breath.

Pulling back to look into her eyes, he brushed her hair away from her face. "I didn't come here to seduce you. I came here to talk. But I want you, Brooke, so much I can't think straight. But I won't push."

Hunger flashed in her big, blue eyes as she stared at his lips. "This connection feels real. It's so raw and honest."

"I agree. Can we start over?" He smiled and reached for her hand. "Hi, I'm Nico. It's a pleasure to meet you."

"Likewise. I'm Brooke." He kissed her hand and her wrist.

"I've been hard all morning thinking about you," he said on a ragged breath. "Are you sore?"

Her pupils dilated. "Yes, but in a good way."

He got to his feet and pulled her up with him, wrapping a hand around her waist. "Work was torture. I couldn't stop thinking about you." He angled his head and pressed his lips to hers. The warmth of her mouth fired his blood.

Her hands wrapped around his neck. Her tongue tangled with his in deep, velvet strokes. A soft whimper escaped from her throat. He angled his head, deepening the kiss, tasting her sweetness.

His mouth moved to her throat and then her neck. "I want you, Brooke, right here, right now." Cupping her breast through her shirt, he rubbed his thumb over her nipple. He glanced over at her desk stacked with books and what looked like tarot cards and thought about taking her right there.

"I want you too," she murmured, breathless, and grabbed his hand. "Let's get out of here."

"I have a better idea, you naked beneath me, bent over the desk and moaning my name." His need for her overwhelmed him. His head swam.

A wave of longing nailed him in the chest. "I want to be sweet and tender, but I'm hanging on by a thread."

Her eyes widened and a lovely pink flush spread from her cheeks to her neck. "We can't. I mean technically we can, but I've never had sex in my office before."

"Now I've gone and scandalized you." He caressed her cheek. The scent of her perfume curled into his senses. "I'd like to be your first." *And you're last.* "The door's locked so no one can barge in, right?"

"Right. But, Nico, you can't be serious. It's so…"

"Spontaneous? Sexy?" He undid the clip in her hair, and her blonde waves tumbled around her shoulders like a golden waterfall. *Damn.* "You're so beautiful. Let me make you feel good. What do you say?"

Her pulse pounded at her throat. Her lips parted. "I say yes."

A dark thrill raced through his blood. "Take your clothes off." His urgent need for her exhilarated him, and scared him all at once, like jumping out of an airplane at twenty-thousand feet. He already had the feeling this thing with Brooke could crush him, wreck him in a way he'd never come back from.

"What are you doing to me, Nico Denopoulos? Although I'm not surprised your Venus moon is a hotbed of sexuality." Her soft laughter filled the room and sent his blood thumping. She kicked off her heels and then slipped her top over her head, revealing a red satin bra.

Lust pooled at his groin. "What are the chances you've got on matching panties?"

Her smile widened. "Pretty good." Her fingers moved to the zipper on her skirt, her gaze never leaving his. When she pushed the material down her hips, the sound echoed in the small space, kicking his desire up a notch.

He held out his hand while she stepped out of her skirt and set it on the chair. She turned back to face him and unhooked her bra, freeing her breasts. He brushed a thumb over one taut nipple, mesmerized by the blonde goddess standing before him.

"You take my breath away."

"You're such a sweet talker."

"It's the truth."

He kicked off his shoes and then shoved his T-shirt over his head. Her warm gaze trailed over his chest and his stomach. The naked desire on her face made him glad he went to the gym. His erection throbbed against his boxers as he rid himself of his jeans. He muttered a curse when her warm hand slid inside the waistband. Her hand moved back and forth, slow and torturous, and then she pulled his boxers down his body.

"You're so big and thick. I don't think I could ever get tired of looking at you."

"All the better to give you pleasure, baby."

Bending his head, his mouth fastened to her nipple. He sucked and licked until she whimpered. The smell of her perfume and her musk drove him out of his mind. Her fingers dug into his shoulders, her soft moans filling his ears. He wrapped his arms around her waist just as her knees gave out. "I love getting you wild."

"Don't make me wait," she panted, looking up at him, her eyes now drowsy with lust.

Sliding a finger into the silk of her panties, he found her wet and swollen. He massaged her clit, rubbing back and forth, using his thumb, getting off on her soft little moans of pleasure.

"Don't stop…"

In one tug, he ripped the silk clean off her body. He'd never been swept up by this kind of consuming passion before, but everything about her brought out every one of his primal urges. "I'll buy you new ones."

When she went over to the desk and lifted her ass in the air, his vision blurred. His cock hardened to the point of pain. He thought he might blow his load right then and there.

"You're gorgeous." He put his face to her hot little pussy and lapped her up.

"Nico…please," she moaned. The pleading note in her voice got his dick pulsing, ready to explode.

He sucked on her clit over and over again, using his fingers until she went off in his mouth. While she came down off her orgasm, he reached for a condom from his jeans pocket, glad he brought one along, just in case. Ripping it open, he hurried to sheathe it over his straining cock.

"I need you inside me. Now." Brooke glanced at him over her shoulder. Her chest rose and fell. Desire flashed in her eyes.

"You don't need to ask twice." He couldn't believe he got to have her again. Lifting her hips, he plunged inside. They both gasped in pleasure at the same time." He moved in and out of her, slow at first. He thought he'd be less desperate the second time around. But he'd been wrong. He slid in deeper, driving into her soaking heat. He nipped her ear and bit her shoulder.

Their breaths mingled together and filled the small room. "You're going to make me come again."

The sound of his name on her lips made his balls ache. He moved faster. "I can feel you, Brooke. Come for me again." He reached for her breast, pinched her nipple, and then slapped her ass, hard.

"Ouch." Her head snapped around. "What was that for?"

"For running away from me." He rubbed her clit to ease the sting.

"I'm close." Her hips arched up and then she clenched all around him, rocking his world. "I'm coming, Nico."

His balls tightened. His cock ached. "That's it. Your pussy is milking every last drop of pleasure out of me." He wrapped her hair around his fist, like he'd been dreaming about doing since day one, and thrust deep. His whole body shook, and then he exploded inside her wet heat. He waited for the aftershocks to pass, and then he kissed her shoulder. "You're incredible. So sweet. Your knees are probably hurting."

"It was worth it," she panted.

After he pulled out of her, he helped her off the desk. Then he tied off the top of the condom, and threw it in the trash. "I'm sorry. I wasn't planning to ravish you at your work." He couldn't wrap his head around how fast and hard he was falling for this woman.

A satisfied smile lit up her striking face. "I'm not complaining. It was hot."

They both dressed, and then he pulled her into his arms and placed a kiss on the top of her head. He'd gotten cynical about love and relationships over the years, until Brooke stepped into his life. And then, "Bam!" he couldn't remember being this happy or excited about life.

Her stomach grumbled. "I've worked up an appetite."

"I bet you haven't eaten all day."

Shaking her head, her gaze filled with remorse. "My stomach was in knots at how I left things with you. I still feel awful about taking off."

"Hey, it's okay." He lifted her chin and caressed her cheek. "This is all happening fast, but how about we navigate things together? No running away, deal?" His chest swelled with an emotion he couldn't identify.

A line formed between her brows, and he suppressed the urge to kiss it away. "I don't know if I can make that promise."

"I'm not going anywhere."

Tears sparked in her eyes. "You don't know how badly I wish that were true."

"What's with the tears, sweetheart?" He wiped them away with his thumb.

She sniffled. "I'm just happy."

Why did he think there was more going on? "Yeah? Me too. When I came into see you, I wasn't just looking for a woman. I was looking for *my* woman. And you're it. I've been thinking about us, and I don't want to sound jealous or possessive, but I don't want to share you with anyone." The thought of her with some other guy was like a vice to the throat. "I know this is crazy. What do you think? Am I going too fast?"

Excitement sparked in her beautiful eyes. "I feel the same way. I don't want to share you with anyone, either."

He sighed, relieved. "Let's go grab a bite. Are you ready for date number two?"

Snuggling into his chest, she rested her head against his heart. "I have a pretty good idea how the date ends."

CHAPTER 9

BROOKE

The next couple of weeks passed in a blur. They'd been the best of Brooke's life and the most excruciating, because now a ticking time bomb hung over their heads. She'd been falling hard and fast for Nico from their first date. And now she couldn't imagine her life without him in it. Their relationship was exhilarating and sensual, everything she'd always dreamed about and more.

Their minds were simpatico, and their lovemaking grew more passionate by the day. Sometimes it was hot and dirty, other times slow and intimate. They spent hours talking about their hopes and dreams, encouraging each other to chase after them. Nico convinced her to write her astrology book, and she gave him ideas for his restaurant expansion. The pull of their lives together in another time and place seemed stronger than ever.

He'd found a way into her heart. And now that sensation filtered through every aspect of her existence, but when summer turned to fall in less than a month, he'd forget all about her. A sick feeling in her stomach spread to her limbs. How would she live without him or go back to her old, lonely existence? She found the other half of her soul in Nico.

Pushing the myriad of doubts to the back of her mind, she kicked off the covers and got out of bed. She went into the bathroom and caught her reflection in the mirror while she brushed her teeth. The dreamy look of satisfaction and bliss on her face caught her off-guard. "I've got it bad," she muttered to her reflection. The end of summer crept closer, like sand slipping through her fingertips

After she showered and dressed, she walked out of her room and stopped on the landing. She stared at the framed portrait of her famous ancestor, Melinda Howe, and placed her hands on her hips. "You're the one that started all the trouble."

For a split second, she swore Melinda smiled back at her. Everyone who saw the portrait said they looked exactly alike. They both shared the same wavy, blonde hair, round blue eyes, and long nose that she'd been teased about growing up. Brooke could see the resemblance and the parallels. "Now my life is about to turn into a total shitshow and all because you pissed off the wrong woman. Hell hath no fury like a witch who's been scorned."

"Talking to yourself again?" Arabella called up from the bottom of the stairs.

Brooke brushed a finger across the edge of the frame. "I was just saying we need to dust more." The echo of voices and footfalls greeted her as she descended the staircase to the main floor.

"Have you told Nico about the curse?" Arabella asked, drawing her brows together.

"I'm planning to tell him at the Founder's Festival." She'd been looking forward to their big Labor Day fling for weeks, but that was before she started dating Nico—before she fell head over heels in love with him. The plan was to meet the other witches in the greenhouse and conjure a spell and a potion to counter the curse before next week's full moon when the magick would be at its peak.

"If the invocation works then maybe there won't be a reason to. It's going to be okay." Arabella touched her arm. "I promise."

Her words soothed some of Brooke's panic. "I pray you're right. I want to believe with all my heart that this time will be different."

A few hours later, Brooke stood in the greenhouse with Arabella, Delilah, and Gillian on one side of her. Ellen, Saje and Willow stood on the other. Seven anointed white candles surrounded them.

Moonlight spilled into the room from the wall of windows and cast an eerie glow above their heads. A tattered ancient grimoire from their library sat in the center on a book stand next to a hand mirror and a smoking cauldron.

"Are you ready, ladies?" Willow asked, trading glances with each of the women. She cleansed the area using salt and a ritual broom. After she finished, she set pink and green votive candles on the flat surface of the mirror.

Ellen, the high priestess of their coven, flicked her wrist and all the candles flamed to life. Lifting her hands, she waved them over the leather-bound tome. "Show me curses." The locks on the ruby encrusted book clicked open. The pages flipped and then stopped on a page filled with flames and hearts. Her gaze moved to Brooke. "You're up, my dear."

Brooke walked around the other ladies pointing the tip of her wand in a clockwise direction until she formed a circle. "I long to be with a man like Nico who understands my mind and fulfills my passions." She silently repeated the words and kept them at the forefront of her mind until she completed the circle.

"Potion time." Saje picked up a copper bowl filled with herbs, then sprinkled them into the cauldron. "Basil for banishment and rose petals for love." She glanced at Brooke. "Do you have your offering?"

Pulling out the blonde and black braid of her and Nico's hair from her pocket brought a smile to Brooke's lips. The contrast made her think of their personalities and filled her heart with warmth.

"I snipped it while he was asleep. I'm not proud of myself." Guilt slid in her belly. "I hate keeping secrets from him." But it was the only way to invoke the counter-spell to break the curse once and for all. Closing her fingers over the braid, images of Nico kissing her and making her laugh filled her head. She held on tighter. What if it didn't work? Her head spun. She found it hard to breathe.

"Easy there." Gillian pried the braid from her white-knuckled grip.

Brooke swallowed hard and tossed the braid into the cauldron. Flames shot in the air. "He's the first guy that made me feel like I'm enough."

"Of course you're enough. But even if you did tell him, do you think he'd believe you?" Gillian's concerned gaze narrowed in her direction. "It's not every day you find out the woman you're dating has been hexed with a generational curse."

A sigh of frustration fell from Brooke's lips. Her past now reared up to haunt her and destroy her relationship. "Thanks for the reminder, cuz."

"Why don't you start us off, Brooke?" Willow asked, breaking through the heaviness in the room.

"Right." Her stomach twisted into knots. Pulling out the copy of the spell she'd written from the inside of her bra, she kept the slip of paper close to her heart. She closed her eyes and took several deep breaths.

"Through flame and flare I dissolve this curse forever.

The love in my heart will be the true measure.

I want to let go of the sins of the past

And move forward with the new spell I cast.

This is my will, so mote it be."

One by one, all of the witches joined hands. They repeated the words over and over again, until the room vibrated with energy.

The air hummed with sparks of magick. Brooke silently prayed with everything in her for the incantation to work its way through time and space. Pink and green smoke billowed out of the cauldron and circled around the room.

"Time to drink this bad boy." Saje picked up the ladle from the pedestal and plunged it into the smoking cauldron. She used a sieve to strain the bubbling concoction into a mason jar. After she finished, she handed the potion to Brooke and smiled. "Bottoms up."

"Here's to your health." Brooke downed the potion in one gulp. *Big mistake.* The liquid burned her throat and made her gag. She coughed, hoping she didn't puke. "How will I know if it worked?"

"You just go right up to that gorgeous man of yours, tell him you're nuts about him and lay one on him. You'll know, honey; believe me, you'll know. I'm betting he feels the same way," Ellen said with a wink. Her words lifted the heaviness in the air.

Brooke laughed. "I can't wait to see Nico and test your theory." *Could I finally be free?*

"Let's clean up and go celebrate." When Willow lifted the cauldron, she sucked in a harsh breath. She squeezed her eyes shut. After several agonizing minutes, her eyes flew open wide. She turned to Brooke and shook her head. "I just had a premonition of you on the balcony of your room crying. All the leaves on the trees had changed color. I'm so sorry, Brooke, but the spell didn't take."

Brooke's stomach dropped. "I thought it was too good to be true."

Rushing to her side, Gillian touched her arm. "You can't give up. We're going to find a way to break the curse and let you live a normal life."

"That's all I ever wanted. What do you think went wrong?" Brooke glanced over at Willow. "Why didn't the spell take?" The crushing disappointment forced her to fight back tears. She'd been searching for a piece of her that had been missing for years, a constant craving for love and intimacy. She'd finally found it with Nico, and in a matter of a few short weeks, it would be ripped away.

Willow ran a hand through her red hair and shared a look with Gillian. "If I had to guess, I'd say it's because we only used something personal from you and Nico, but nothing from your ancestor, Melinda. I know it's a long shot, but if you could find something that was passed down from her, then we might have a chance."

Tears burned behind Brooke's eyes. "There's only one person alive who may be able to help. I need to pay a visit to my mom. In the meantime, I plan on doing whatever it takes to make sure Nico doesn't forget me."

CHAPTER 10

NICO

"*A*re you enjoying the festival?"

Nico glanced over at Brooke and his chest grew tight. She stood at his food stand under a canopy of fairy lights, eating a cup of chocolate gelato. Wisps of blonde hair came loose from a messy bun. Her Luna Lovegood costume consisted of a form-fitting white top under a black cape and a pair of crazy glasses perched on top of her head.

"How could I not? I'm here with you."

Laughter and shouts boomed over a jazz band playing in the background. Nico turned to the sound, reveling in the spectacle before him. "Welcome to Raven's Hollow" banners hung from every storefront. The sidewalks buzzed with people dressed up as some sort of famous witch or wizard from pop culture. Crowds milled around Washington Street, now cordoned off from traffic. He turned back to face her. His gaze moved over her face, taking in the stress lines around her mouth.

"Let's make the most of this night." Brooke finished her gelato and threw her cup in the trash. Nico picked up on the melancholy in her voice. Something seemed to be bothering her all night.

Closing the distance between them, Nico whispered close to her ear, "Are you okay?" The scent of her perfume flared in his nostrils, reminding him of her naked in his bed tangled up in the sheets. He'd woken up with her breasts cupped in his hand, their legs intertwined like vines. He wanted to get her alone and hold her in his arms again, take the weight of the world off her shoulders.

"I've been meaning to talk to you about something," she said, a sad note to her voice.

"You can tell me anything, Brooke. I'm here for you. What's going on?"

Before she could respond, Gillian walked up wearing a blue, flowy Glinda dress. "Hey, you two." She linked arms with Brooke and smiled at her costume. "I ran into a friend that wants to book you for a sesh. Can I steal her away for a sec, Nico?"

Brooke looked up at Nico with a tentative smile. "Do you mind?"

"Of course not. I need to find Alex anyway. I'll meet you back here in a few." Nico kissed her cheek, turned, and headed in the other direction. He wasn't looking forward to discussing the subject matter with his brother. He'd put off clearing out his uncle's house long enough. Now it was time to take care of business.

Scanning the crowd, he found Alex decked out in a shaggy, black wig and long cloak. He pulled off Hagrid without a hitch. Nico got his attention and waved.

Alex stopped in front of him and pulled him into a man hug. He eased back, nodding his approval. "Good costume."

"You too." Thanks to Brooke, Nico now sported a fake scar on his forehead and a pair of broken glasses. Sweat broke out on his neck from the muggy night air. He rubbed a hand under his collar. "I'm sweating my ass off in this cape."

"You and me both. Here's the plan. I spoke to the lawyer, and he says we need to go to Uncle George's house by the end of the week and clear it out before the auctioneer stops by. After that, the realtor can put it on the market." Alex patted him on the back. "I get this will be hard for you, but it's time."

"I still can't believe Uncle George is gone." Saying the words out loud felt like a sucker punch to the gut. He'd always been his biggest cheerleader. "Let me know the day and time that works for you, and I'll be there."

"Will do. I need to go find Willow. I'll catch up with you later."

After Nico shook his brother's hand, he walked back through the crowd and found Brooke back at his food stand. "Let's go somewhere private where we can talk." Taking her hand, Nico laced their fingers together.

"I've got just the place." Brooke pointed in the opposite direction, away from the commotion.

They cut across Washington Street, passing the old clock tower now decked out with balloons. The warm summer night surrounded them like a cocoon as they walked along the moon-drenched path to Elysian Park.

"There's something I want to show you." When they got to the entrance, they walked to a secluded area of the park. They stopped at a copse of towering trees. He looked up at the largest one he'd ever seen. Twisted branches loomed overhead, creating a canopy above them.

He pointed to the tree and whistled. "Pretty impressive." The night came alive with the chirp of crickets. The bushes blinked with fireflies. The heavy scent of pine filled the air.

"This is the Hollow Oak." Brooke pressed her hand against the bark. "It's an enchanted tree that some believe makes wishes come true." The sweet sound of her voice lulled him like a siren's call.

"An enchanted tree?" Nico chuckled at the whimsy.

She bumped his shoulder. "It's true. This is the oldest tree in Raven's Hollow and there's a legend surrounding it."

Pushing a loose strand of hair behind her ear, he ran his fingers over the elegant column of her neck. He took off his glasses and shoved them in the front pocket of his shirt, giving her his full attention. "By all means, indulge me with the legend." He'd never bought into the myth and lore surrounding the town before, but the way her eyes lit up made him curious.

A breath fell from her lips like she might reveal some deep, dark secret. "If you stand under the tree when the moon is full and make a wish, your wish will come true. This tree is special to me. My family has a connection to it that goes back generations."

"Does this have anything to do with what's been bothering you all night?" He caressed her cheek.

"Yes." She gave him a sorrowful smile. "I don't know where to start. This is about us...about our relationship."

"Talk to me, Brooke." He pressed a kiss to her temple. "There's not a soul around. We have this whole place to ourselves."

"Do you see those initials?" She angled her head to the center of the tree.

If he squinted, he could pick up the faint traces of the letters L&M in a heart. "Who were they?"

"Melinda was my ancestor. She's a descendant of Elizabeth Howe, one of the women put to death during the Salem Witch Trials."

"I'm sorry. I didn't know." He put his arm around her shoulder and pulled her close. "I read about the trials, but I didn't make the connection with your last name."

"Witches flocked to this town from Salem and the British equivalent—Boscastle, England—to avoid persecution." Pulling away, she turned back to the tree, tracing a finger over the heart. "Melinda came here with her family to the first Founder's Festival and crossed paths with a handsome stranger named Lucas. He saved her from a horse and buggy coming down the street and the two fell madly in love." Her voice lapsed into a dreamy cadence that lulled him deeper into the story.

"It sounds like love at first sight." If Melinda looked anything like Brooke, then Nico could relate. The first time they'd met, she'd blindsided him with her beauty and wit. He leaned against the tree, and he swore he'd been in this exact spot with Brooke before. He shook his head to dispel the odd sensation.

"Lucas was promised to another from birth, so they were forced to meet in secret, and correspond through letters. This is where they shared their first kiss." Turning back to face him, Brooke parted her lips. She released a whispery breath that got his heart thumping.

"Sounds romantic. Was there a happy ending to their story?" he asked, enthralled by the tale of lovers and the catch in her voice.

"I'm afraid not. Melinda was forced to go into hiding with her family when she found out she was pregnant. She delivered her baby in secret. Lucas eventually found out and forged a plan for them to leave the baby with relatives, so they could meet at the tree and run away together."

"What about their baby?"

"They planned to come back for her after they were married to avoid a scandal and the risk of her being taken away."

"Let me guess, they never did?" He massaged her neck, mesmerized by the way history came alive in her imagination.

"No," she said in a sad voice. "An unexpected summer storm rolled in. They were struck down by lightning."

"How tragic," he murmured, moved by the tale of love and loss.

"Legend says, every year if you come to this tree after midnight on Founder's Day, you can still hear Melinda and Lucas calling to each other, trying to run to the tree." The rapture in her voice warmed his blood. Telling the tale of lost lovers suffused the night with romance.

His thumb brushed her bottom lip. "I still don't get what this has to do with us."

"The woman Lucas was supposed to marry was a witch. She wanted revenge for his betrayal and put a curse on my bloodline." Brooke blinked and her eyes filled with tears. "Now every woman on my mother's side is doomed when it comes to love. It can never last."

Though he tried not to react, her words hit him in the gut. "I'd be the first one to say I don't know much about witchcraft, but a curse?" He'd grown cynical about love after his divorce. Then he met Brooke and his whole outlook shifted. His world changed.

"You have to trust me, Nico, this is real. It's one of the reasons I became a matchmaker, to match other people up because love never works out for me."

"I do trust you...with my life, and I respect your beliefs." Tilting her chin up, the sight of her tears hit him like a sucker-punch. "The woman I know doesn't let some legend dictate how she lives her life. She squeezes out every last drop."

Tears ran down her cheeks. "I put all my faith in the stars and magick. I take things like curses very seriously."

"I can't bear to see you cry. We've all had bad breakups, sweetheart." Nico wiped her tears away with his thumb. "That doesn't mean you're cursed."

"When the season changes, so will your feelings."

"What are you talking about? I'm not going anywhere, unless you don't feel the same way." The thought was too terrible to bear. "When I'm with you, it's a perpetual state of freefall. The more time I spend with you, the more I never want to be away." He'd been falling for her fast and hard since day one. He brushed her hair away from her face and kissed her forehead.

"These last few weeks have been the best of my life," she said in a shaky voice.

"Mine too. I miss you when we're not together. It's agony when you leave. You're all I think about, and you're everything I've ever wanted in a partner. It may be too soon to say this, but I think I'm falling in love with you." Who was he kidding? He was already there. From the moment they started dating, everything changed. It wasn't a slide into love but a full-on plummet, which made a hell of a lot of sense because she was smart, caring, gorgeous, and awesome in every way possible.

More tears fell to her cheeks. "I...only wish things were different. The sad truth is this relationship won't last."

"Baby, stop talking like that. You're scaring me. What I feel for you isn't going to change when the leaves fall to the ground." Nico pressed her hand to his heart where it pounded in his chest.

"You don't understand. This curse is cruel and powerful enough to break the hearts of all the females in my family descended from Melinda's bloodline."

A host of nagging questions filtered through his head. "You're saying there's a cosmic conspiracy against you and your family? What makes you think this curse is real and not bad luck?" He stroked her hair, trying to ease her fears.

Her watery gaze met his. "For years I attracted the worst kind of men. But then more recently I started to attract some normal ones, but they act like they don't know who I am by the next equinox." The rawness in her voice struck him like a knife to the chest.

"It sounds like you dated a batch of a-holes. They didn't know what they had, but I do. And I'm grateful to each and every one of them because that's what brought me to you." His gut clenched from the torment she endured.

Standing on her tiptoes, she placed her hand on his chest, right above his heart. "I love your optimism. But you have to hear the extent of it. My mother's destiny has been to cheat on every man she's ever loved. Her mother was married multiple times because her husbands all fell out of love with her. My great grandmother's husband deserted her and their eight young children for another woman."

"I'm sorry. That's awful. I see how much this has affected you." He took her hand and placed a kiss on the inside of her palm with all the tenderness now crushing his ribcage. "It seems we both have jagged edges, but we can't let them rule our lives. Nothing's going to change the way I feel about you. I promise, we'll figure this out together."

CHAPTER 11

BROOKE

*B*rooke's stomach fluttered from the conviction in Nico's words. "Thanks for listening. It's such a relief to finally tell you the truth."

"I hate that you carry this burden around with you every day." He wrapped his hand around her waist. From the way he listened, Brooke could tell he wanted to know every secret, every dark shadow about her, and that gave her hope.

"I guess I've gotten used to it by now." Brooke exhaled a shaky breath. "Once the curse is broken, then Melinda and Lucas can be together forever, and all of her female descendants will be free. Everyone says I'm the spitting image of her. I get these flickers of memory from another time. And I've always been terrified of storms for as long as I can remember."

"And you believe your fear of storms is linked to Melinda dying in one?"

She nodded. "I've been having these dreams about getting caught in a storm since I was a child. Over the past few weeks, they've become more vivid." On the nights she stayed at his place, she'd been waking up shaking with the sound of wind and rain still pounding in her ears.

He placed a sweet kiss on her cheek. "Jesus, Brooke. I feel terrible. You should've woken me up, so I could've been there for you."

His words made her melt. "I think I'm reliving the storm because I was Melinda in a past life."

He rubbed the back of his head with doubt clouding his eyes. "I admit it's kind of eerie that you look just like Melinda. What about Lucas? What did he look like?"

"I've always wondered. I've searched all the historical registries for years and never found anything. I don't even know his last name."

"Have you talked to your mom about all this?"

Her stomach dropped. "I haven't seen her in a while. She was having an affair while she was married to my dad. Her infidelity destroyed him and broke up our family. She left when my younger brother Drew and I were young. When that relationship ended, she was onto the next one." The pain dulled over time like a scab over an open wound.

"I'm sorry, Brooke." His gaze pierced hers, and genuine sincerity burned in his eyes.

"We don't speak much anymore. It must be hard for you to understand, coming from a loving family."

"I can't imagine how hard that must've been for you," he whispered, rubbing her back.

The weight of his concern allowed her to continue. "It was more difficult for Drew. We made it through, but I still have the battle scars." *Everyone leaves.*

"You deserve love, and all the happiness in the world."

"I don't know what a happily-ever-after looks like, Nico. My parents fought all the time." The admission sparked a host of ugly memories. "I used to hide in my room with my hands over my ears, praying to be anywhere but there."

"I wish I could take that pain away from you." Pressing his hands on her shoulders, she leaned into his warmth. "If I could, I would, but it's what made you the strong, incredible woman you are today."

Her heart somersaulted from his praise. "I took her rejection hard. I still struggle with self-doubt and feeling like I'm not good enough." Talking about this gut-wrenching subject with Nico lifted some of the hurt away.

"You don't have to feel that way anymore. I'm here. I've got you." He pulled her against the hard wall of his chest and wrapped her in his arms. She found comfort in his masculine scent and the steady beat of his heart.

Several minutes ticked by. When she finally pulled back and looked up at his handsome face, some of her tension had melted away. All her secrets had been laid out bare. Her heart and soul stretched out before him. No more hiding. No more shame.

He traced the space between her brows with the pad of his finger. "What's this about? Tell me what you're thinking right now."

"The curse compelled my mom into the arms of another man, but not keeping in touch with her children…that's on her." And then those same nagging fears and doubts flitted through her head, leaving her shaken and sick with dread. "What if I'm like her? What if that kind of detachment is genetic, something that burns in the veins?"

"You're not like her. I know you. You're warm and loving. You'd never leave your family." Nico believed in Brooke even when she didn't believe in herself. A bittersweet tenderness filled her, lifting the darkness that lived inside her by exposing it to light.

"Admitting this out loud and not having you judge me means everything."

"A hurt that deep can hollow you out if you let it." He kissed her temple and her eyelids, whispering words of sweet encouragement.

Her heart soared, tripping over every word. "Tonight, when I look up into the sky, I want to imagine we can rearrange the stars."

"Me too, sweetheart. Me too." He trailed his fingers up and down her arms, leaving a trail of heat and longing in their wake.

She loved that he couldn't seem to stop touching her. Stars twinkled overhead and gave off a starry effect, drawing her gaze up to a full moon. Fireworks went off, adding to the dreamlike quality of the night. Bursts of red, gold, and silver magic flared.

Pointing to the blasts, Nico looked up. "It's a gorgeous night. We're supposed to be having fun, remember?"

"I want to bask in this moment." Sharing secrets reinforced their connection and made them stronger. She wanted to lose herself in this man and not think about what might happen tomorrow. "The fates have kept me from living my desires, until now."

"What do you wish for?"

"I wish we could stay right here and hold each other, shut out the rest of the world. What about you?" She toyed with the string at his collar. Maybe it was being here with Nico, the excitement of the fireworks, and the soft breeze lifting his hair off his collar, but it felt like nothing bad could happen.

"I wish I could make love to you right here at this tree under the stars with the backdrop of fireworks," he said close to her ear.

Her heart swelled with the romance of the idea. A soft hum of need prickled beneath her skin. Nico could worship her body and stimulate her mind. And then it hit her with the force of a shooting star. *How much I love Nico*. The thought made her breathe too hard. Terror overshadowed her joy. Her time with him was almost coming to an end. Her world turned on its axis. She swayed on her feet.

He caught her around the waist. "Whoa, steady there. Are you okay?"

"It must be all the excitement. I got dizzy for a moment."

"Hold onto me. I won't let you fall."

Happy tears pricked at her eyes. "Make love to me, Nico, right here under the stars. I can't think of anything more romantic." Loving him might be the scariest thing she'd ever done.

His face lit up as bright as the blasts exploding all around them. He didn't answer her with words. Bending his head, he kissed her, long and deep. His tongue tangled with hers in lush, velvety strokes. The kiss raged on, wet and searing hot. Then Brooke was drowning in heat and taste infused from the past.

Could they have been touched by destiny?

When his hand trailed up her thigh and reached under her skirt to her panties, she gasped. He pulled the lace aside and pushed his finger into her aching core. The pad of his thumb massaged her clit, adding the perfect amount of pressure. Her head fell back on a moan.

"You're so soft and already wet for me." The raw need in his voice ignited her passion.

"I want you, Nico." Sweat misted on her skin from his touch and the humid night air. Her sex rippled beneath his stroking fingers, pushing her to orgasm.

"I've got to get you ready first." He gave her a look that promised sinful things to come. He added a second finger and rubbed back and forth. Flames of heat licked across her sensitized flesh. Her whole body trembled with need when he pulled his fingers out and slowly thrust them back into her, circling her clit in a steady, mindless rhythm. Tiny explosions of pleasure erupted under her skin.

Her back bowed against the tree. Panting hard, she lifted her hips against the onslaught of pleasure cresting over her, ignoring the fact that her skirt bunched up to her waist. Her core tightened as her climax raced over her, leaving her breathless.

"I want to take those tragic memories and turn them into something beautiful." His sweet words tightened her chest. The way he looked at her made her feel special, sexy, and wanted in the most exquisite way. She soaked up every detail of this moment and locked it away to cherish forever.

Bursts of color continued to saturate the sky and mingled with the magic of the night. She reached for him, stroking his erection through his jeans. Together, they undid his belt buckle, and she freed his cock from the waistband of his boxer-briefs. He grew rock hard in her hand as she rubbed him from base to tip and back again.

"I want to be buried deep inside you, but I don't have a condom," he said in a hoarse voice and pressed his forehead to hers.

"It's okay. I trust you, and I'm on the pill." Her body hummed and softened as it molded to his.

"The best wishes really do come true," he groaned. "I can't wait to feel you skin to skin with no barrier between us. I'm beginning to believe in this tree legend after all."

"I told you." She smiled as tenderness warmed her heart.

"I don't want the bark to rub against your back." Before she could protest, in one quick move, he switched their positions, so he leaned against the tree.

Her body was strung tight. She needed all of him—his cock, his fingers, and his mouth.

After he helped her step out of her panties, he shoved them in the front pocket of his shirt. He scooted himself down so their bodies aligned, and then he pulled his cape around them. "I knew this damn thing would come in handy for something."

She laughed, and rubbed up against him, breathing hard. "I need you." Their hips bumped and she gasped. He lifted her leg and then in one deep thrust, he slid inside her, bursting through her, stripping her of thought.

He moved back and forth, slow and sensual, filling every inch of her, making her forget the rest of the world existed. His tall frame trembled as every searing inch of him filled her.

The way he gazed into her eyes, breathing the same air, got her heart hammering away in her chest. Only a man as sensual as Nico could satisfy her deepest desires, and feed her soul. She loved every minute of their lovemaking. She never imagined sex could be like this.

"You're mine." Picking up the pace, he slid in deeper, growing thicker. This felt like a claiming, a merging of the souls. The way his eyes darkened with need and affection broke through her last remaining barrier. Tears burned in her eyes as they moved together, in tune to each other's bodies.

Brooke wanted to stay locked in the passion of his embrace and not think about the future. No matter how much she wished for a forever with Nico, their relationship could only be ephemeral.

"You feel so good." His cock rubbed over her clit over and over again, driving her out of her mind.

"Jesus, Brooke, you own me."

His words flayed her open, shattered through her protective walls. Heat crawled up her spine as ecstasy took hold. A swirl of color exploded behind her eyes. "I'm coming." Her orgasm rippled through her limbs like a warm, flowing wave.

"Ah…baby." And then his groan filled the air. His liquid heat filled her, and the hunger built again, spurring another orgasm.

His broad chest heaved with heavy breaths as he buried his face in her neck and held her tight. "You're incredible. I'm so glad I found you."

"Me, too." A warm contentment spread throughout her body. Happiness like she'd never known filled the cracks in her heart. She wanted to tell him that she loved him, but it was too soon.

"Are you ready to get out of here, or do you want to head back to the festival?" He pulled up his pants, still breathing hard and fast.

"I'd like to spend the rest of the evening making love to you in a bed." She adjusted her skirt and then wrapped her arms around his neck. She never imagined sex could go from being hot and dirty one minute, to sweet and intimate the next.

Placing a kiss on her lips, he pulled her close. "I think that can be arranged. You can be sure of one thing, curses be damned. I'm not going anywhere."

CHAPTER 12

BROOKE

*T*he drive to her mother's house in Croton took just under an hour with traffic. Brooke didn't bother to call beforehand. She just showed up. This couldn't wait. After she got out of her car, she swallowed hard against the butterflies floating around in her stomach.

Her mother's old, white Volkswagen sat in the driveway. *Good, at least she's home.* Brooke didn't know how Sarah would feel about her stopping by unannounced, but it would be worth it if she got answers.

A cool breeze caressed her skin, taunting her with the implication of summer ending and fall rolling in. The clock was ticking. When a stray leaf floated through the air and landed at her feet, she figured it must be a sign. The threat of the season changing twisted around her neck like a vice.

She rang the doorbell and tapped her foot as she waited. Eventually, she gave up and figured she'd try out back. The soft notes of wind chimes clinked together. Their music floated through the air as she came around the side of the house, passing rows of lavender, bursting sunflowers, and night-blooming jasmine. Their scents mingled together, perfuming the air, filling her head with a hotbed of painful memories. She spotted her mom sitting at a green wrought iron table in the center of the garden, flipping through a deck of tarot cards. Seven lit votive candles and a crystal sat in the center of the table.

Her mother's hand stilled as she lifted a card, and then she turned to face Brooke. A surprised smile spread across her face. "Brooke? I saw that a loved one was going to pay me a visit. I'm preparing for a client." Sarah motioned to her tarot deck. "It's been a long time. I'm glad you're here."

What did one say to a mother who had only seen her kids a handful of times in the past seven years? She'd missed out on birthdays, homework, plays, football games, and both her and Drew's graduations from high school and college. "Hello" didn't seem appropriate. Sadness leaked into Brooke's heart for all those lost years. She sucked air into her lungs and breathed through the sudden well of emotion. Why wasn't Brooke enough for her mom to stay? She knew the answer. She could chalk it up to the curse.

"It's good to see you, Mom."

Everyone said they shared the same eyes, but her mother's seemed colder and filled with a lifetime's worth of pain.

"You, too." Her mother's voice tugged Brooke out of the past. "Come in and sit down. How about some iced tea? I could go inside and make us a pitcher."

"Thanks, I'm good." Brooke's mind drifted to the day her mother left as she walked across the lawn and sat down at the table on one of the garden chairs. School had just ended, which meant the official start of summer. She'd worn the blue and yellow halter dress, Brooke's favorite. When she came down the stairs, clutching her suitcases, Brooke knew in her heart that she wouldn't be coming back. Painful memories from that day still haunted her like ghosts. Tamping down the ache inside her, she cleared her throat and set her keys on the table.

"Have you eaten? I could heat up some leftover stew. I made up a batch and dropped some off at the foodbank." The Aquarius in Sarah gave freely to the world, just not to her own family. As her mom pushed her astrology wheel to the side, her rose perfume drifted in the air, stirring another flash of memory. Brooke beat back the remnants from the past and focused on what she came here to do.

"Thanks, but I'm not hungry." Brooke's stomach twisted. They made small talk for a while and then her mom flipped a card from her tarot deck. "The Ace of Wands. It looks like business is going well." Her mother looked up and cocked her head to the side. "How's Drew?"

"He's doing well. He got his first job out of college. You'd know that if you called him more."

"You're right. I should." Sarah sighed. "And I regret letting so much time pass. I'm proud of both of my children."

Brooke's anger flared. "You have a funny way of showing it." She bit down on her lip. Her and Drew went to see her here on weekends after she left. She'd call and write letters, but over the years, the visits and calls eventually stopped. The rejection never failed to chafe. The hurt of her mother leaving when she needed her the most still lingered.

"I guess I've made a real mess of things." Regret flickered in her mother's eyes.

"Why didn't you come back for us?"

"At first, I was ashamed of how I left things. I kept thinking I'd come back and everything would be okay, but too much time had gone by. That old life...well...it was too confining for me."

Brooke snorted. "While you were living on your own and finding yourself, I took on the role of parent to a lost, angry teenager." Drew had started getting wasted on school nights until she'd stepped in. She'd stayed home every weekend her entire senior year to keep him out of trouble. Memories from that awful time washed over her and left her reeling. The sacrifice of missing out on prom and parties seemed trivial when she thought about what could've happened. Eventually, Drew grew up and graduated college with an engineering degree. They survived, despite their mother abandoning them.

"I feel awful about that. If I could go back and change things, I would, but I can't. Fate doesn't always follow what's in the deepest recesses of our hearts, Brooke. Our charts hold the answers."

"I'm not here to discuss the meaning behind our charts. I'm here because I have questions about Melinda. Do you have anything of hers? An heirloom? Anything at all?"

"You've tried to break the curse?"

She sighed deep. "Dozens of times, but so far nothing seems to work. I've just experienced a few setbacks. There must be another way." Brooke refused to give up hope. She couldn't lose Nico, not now, not when she'd just found him.

"I do have something of hers, but don't count on it to break the curse. I should know. I've tried." Her mother's voice filled with sadness.

"I need to try this for myself, Mom. Please, I'm begging you." Brooke's voice grew thick with unshed tears.

"I don't want to see you suffer the same fate." Her eyes softened. "But I can see you're determined. I'll be right back."

While her mother got up from the table and went into the side door of the house, Brooke lifted her chin, soaking up the last remnants of afternoon sunshine. Her gaze swept over the garden. A tree stump adorned with flowers, candles and bundles of herbs caught her eye. Why did her mom have an altar out here?

The back door opened and closed, and then her mother reappeared, holding a stack of envelopes tied with tattered ribbons. The edges of the paper had yellowed and frayed. "These belonged to Melinda. They're her correspondence with Lucas."

Brooke's heart fluttered in her chest as she took the stack from her mother's outstretched hands. "Melinda's love letters? How in the world did you get these?"

"They were passed down from generation to generation. I got them from your grandmother."

"How come you never showed them to me before?"

"You never asked." Her mother touched her arm. "I don't think you've ever been in love before, not like this anyway. I see it in your eyes. But I warn you to be cautious. Love will only bring you down and destroy you. Trust me, I speak from experience."

"Please, don't." Brooke held up her hand. "I'm not giving up because of what happened to you or our family."

"I understand your conviction better than anyone, but even if you find some type of magick to counter the curse, it will manifest in another way," her mother said, shaking her head. "I'm sorry for being cynical, but if you truly love this man then you need to let him go. Otherwise, you're not being fair to him."

A sick misery spread through her limbs. "I have to go." Brooke would find a way to break the cycle for everyone's sake. She refused to give up.

They walked to the edge of the grass, and her mom pointed to the altar in the garden. "I do an offering of my flowers to the goddess every day to clear my karma and to ask for forgiveness from everyone I've hurt. I want to ask it from you, Brooke. I'd like to mend our relationship."

"Some things are too broken to mend." Then Brooke remembered Nico's analogy about drinking poison and expecting someone else to die. "But holding onto anger and resentment is no way to live. How about this, I'll give it some thought. Thank you for these." She pressed the letters to her chest and crossed the yard. Her thoughts scattered in a million different directions.

Her mother's words had stirred up her worst fears. The moment Brooke hopped into her car and shut the door, she let the tears fall.

CHAPTER 13

NICO

*a*n uneasy sensation followed Nico throughout the day. Maybe it was this impending storm he kept hearing about on the news, but everything seemed to go wrong from the second he stepped into the restaurant. The dishwasher never showed. Their fresh mozzarella delivery got delayed. A party of eight showed up with fifteen people demanding a table. They were slammed with reservations and short-staffed.

Only the thought of seeing Brooke after closing got him through the chaos. Last night when she told him about the curse, she looked wrecked. Her strength and vulnerability shook him to his core. Every time his mind drifted to her, this insatiable need to talk to her—and make love to her, tugged at his head and his heart.

How could he convince her that he wanted something long-term? He didn't know how to console her or convince her that his feelings were real and not about to change from the power of some ancient hex. Then it hit Nico right between the eyes, blindsiding him with the force of the revelation. He was deeply, madly in love with Brooke Howe.

BROOKE

The banging on her bedroom door barely registered. Brooke had been sprawled out on her bed with the letters and a magnifying glass from the moment she'd gotten home. She'd spent hours reading about Lucas and Melinda's ill-fated love affair. Her heart bled for them.

Another bang sounded.

Nico! Jolting out of bed, she rushed to the door. She'd gotten so caught up in reading the letters, she'd lost track of time. She opened the door and found him standing on the other side, his stance tense.

"You haven't answered my calls or my texts. We were supposed to meet at my place an hour ago. I got worried. I wanted to make sure you were okay." The way he looked at her with such reverence made her throat dry.

"I'm so sorry, Nico. I got distracted." Brooke ushered him inside her room and shut the door, motioning to the letters. "I paid a visit to my mom today." She grabbed his hand and led him to the edge of her bed. The mattress dipped as he sat down on the end.

"Let me guess, love letters from your high school boyfriend?" Rubbing his hands up and down her arms, he placed a long, deep kiss on her lips, leaving her breathless. When he pulled back, an emotion she couldn't identify burned in his eyes.

"Good guess, but not quite." After she reached for one of the letters, she curled up beside him and handed him the one she'd just read. "Now you have proof that Melinda and Lucas's relationship was real and not some urban love legend."

Lifting the magnifying glass to his eye, he stared at the bold, masculine strokes of calligraphy on the page like he'd seen them before. Was he experiencing the same sudden sense of déjà vu as Brooke? He shook head as though coming out of a daze and began to read the words aloud.

"The river's overflowing and water is rising. I cannot bear to be away from you anymore, Melinda. I have not stopped fighting against my parents' wishes to marry Cassandra. I refuse to spend my days and nights with a woman I do not love." Nico's deep velvet voice lulled Brooke closer.

She listened, captivated, while he read, as though a part of her was recalling a memory she'd buried long ago. Could she and Nico be Melinda and Lucas's reincarnated souls? Her whole body burned with the realization.

"Have you received my letters? I send a messenger every day with one. You should be here with me. My heart is breaking. The storm is upon us, but my pending nuptials grow near. We must run away together tonight and leave our babe behind. You are to be mine. I will meet you at the Hollow Oak at midnight.

"I need to hear you declare your love for me. When I look up into the sky fear swirls all around me, along with the heavy gusts of wind. I am praying for us to ride out the storm in the shelter of the cottage until The Providence can sail us somewhere far away. I will be sending a horse and carriage to fetch you. My only hope is that it brings you to me, my darling. Without you I will die.

Yours forever,

Lucas,"

Nico finished reading, and looked up. "I can't believe these exist." Shock crossed his face as he set the magnifying glass and letter down on her bed. "But this doesn't prove there's a curse on you, Brooke." The moment he said the words, the drapes rustled open at the window, revealing a dark, cloudy sky.

An icy chill settled over Brooke, a sign that a storm was brewing. She'd been afraid of storms for as long as she could remember.

"Then why the strong reaction to the letter?" Brooke turned back to face Nico and couldn't tear her gaze away from the naked emotions in his eyes.

"I don't know," he whispered close to her ear. "I feel like I know these two for some strange reason. It's sad." His gaze kept returning to the letter like he'd been recalling a memory.

"You, me, the impending storm, and the change of season—it's like history repeating itself all over again." A kind of wistful sadness welled up inside her. Maybe her punishment in this life was payment for what she did in another as Melinda.

His jaw clenched. "Except I'm not promised to anyone else and the only one I want is you. I don't believe the fate of our relationship rests in the cosmos."

"I get that this is a lot to take in, but this affects you too. There's something you should know—something that I should've told you from the start."

"Talk to me, Brooke."

Her hand flew to his, and squeezed, not sure how he'd react. "I never mentioned it, because I wasn't sure if you were open to the idea, but the South Node on your birth chart shows you've experienced at least one past life."

"A past life?" he repeated, looking shell-shocked.

"What if you and I…if we…?"

His jaw visibly clenched. "Are two reincarnated souls searching for each other?"

"Yes," she whispered. "But the curse has kept us apart."

Aggravation and frustration hardened his features. "I think you're clinging onto this curse business because you're scared. You don't believe you deserve a happy ending, but that's where you're wrong, Brooke. You deserve everything. Dammit, we both do." When he closed his eyes, she sensed his torment.

These last few weeks she thought she'd been making *some* headway against her fate, but it had all been an illusion. Nico was spending all his time with her when he could be out there finding someone to share his future with. She couldn't keep toying with his heart. It wasn't fair, not after everything he'd been through. There was only one thing she could do.

"I promised I'd find you your soulmate. And I will. But it's not me." Her words lingered in the air and strangled her breath.

"Of course, it's you. It has always been you." The fierceness in his voice froze her in place. "I was planning to ask you to move in with me. I was afraid you might think it was too soon, but now…"

Coldness seeped into her bones. Brooke should've known better than to get this attached because right now something inside her was breaking. "I won't ask you to put your life on hold while I try to figure this thing out. What if I can't?" Tears burned in her eyes. All she ever wanted was passion, love, and stability in her life. Nico gave her that and more. She'd never felt this cherished before.

The way he looked at her sliced her heart in two. "Don't do this, Brooke." His voice rose. "You have free will to make your own decisions. Only you can control your destiny and what's in your heart."

"Yes, but I don't want to take the risk with yours for my own selfish reasons. It wouldn't be fair to you." Emptiness pressed down on her chest, robbing her of breath.

Frustration sparked in his gaze. "You're going to give up that easily?" The words stung like a physical ache. "That's not the woman I've come to know and care for."

"Nico, I...can't." Her voice broke.

"You didn't let what your mother did break you because you're strong and resilient. You can't let this belief in some supernatural force come between us." Anger colored his face and edged back into his voice as he got to his feet.

"Don't go, not like this," she whispered, and her heart broke a little more. The season would change, and she'd never see him again. This couldn't be happening.

"I won't play this game with you, Brooke. I love you. Do you hear me? I love you. I love everything about you, your sharp mind and your fascination with astrology and your sweetness. I want to share my life with you. I want to be there when you're happy or sad. I want to be all in for the long-haul." He looked lost and wounded.

"I only wish I could promise you something that will last." Pulling her knees to her chest, she stared at his face, committing every detail to memory.

"Bullshit. You're pulling away from me, and it hurts."

"The last thing I ever want to do is hurt you, which is why I have to let you go." The words exploded from Brooke's chest. All the happiness she'd been feeling these past few weeks shriveled and turned as black as the sky.

"I could chase you and promise you everything, but it won't change a damn thing." The hurt in his voice blistered between them and tore her to shreds. "There are no guarantees in this life...none. When you're ready to hold onto what we have, let me know." Crossing the room to her door, he opened it and walked out of her life.

The finality in his words felt like a crushing blow that shattered her insides. Brooke couldn't move. She couldn't breathe. A sob broke loose. Her heart crumbled into pieces. Tears streamed down her cheeks and splashed onto her neck in big, salty drops. *What have I done?*

Her chest ached with physical pain, and she realized this was what it felt like to have her heart break.

CHAPTER 14

NICO

*L*eaning against the side of his car, Nico regretted how he'd left things with Brooke. He'd never experienced this sense of loss before, even after his divorce.

His phone rang. He lifted it out of his pocket and cursed under his breath when Alex's number flashed across the screen instead of Brooke's. He pressed accept and put the phone to his ear. "What's up?"

"We need to get over to Uncle George's house tomorrow, before the storm hits to make sure the basement doesn't flood and the windows are secure."

"Shit, I almost forgot." His head was all over the place. "I can be there bright and early." He'd welcome the distraction.

"You sound funny. Are you okay?" After Nico released a frustrated breath, he began to process his new reality. And then a wave of emotion knocked him in the head like a right hook. "No. I just lost the love of my life."

BROOKE

"Hey, honey? You need to get out of bed and rejoin the land of the living."

When Brooke looked up, she found Arabella at the end of her bed holding a tray filled with toast, fresh berries, and a mug of tea. Brooke had filled her in on her breakup with Nico after he left. She couldn't seem to stop crying.

Setting the tray down on her nightstand, Arabella walked to the windows and drew the curtains back, revealing the dark, stormy day that mirrored Brooke's mood. She sunk deeper into the pillows, trying to push down the despair wreaking havoc over her heart.

"Staying in this bed isn't going to change anything. Why don't you try and eat something?" Arabella walked back to the side of her bed and motioned to the tray.

"I'm too nauseated to eat, but I love you for trying." She swiped at the tears in her eyes. "I've never been this emotional." When Brooke tried to imagine a life without Nico, a cold malaise settled over her limbs like wet cement. She could chalk it up to another doomed relationship, but not this time. Her heart wouldn't let her. The need to be close to Nico consumed every part of her.

Arabella shoved Brooke's pumps out of the way and took a seat on the bench facing her bed. Brooke's heart swelled with love and gratitude for her friend for sticking by her in the depths of her despair. "What about getting up and trying to do something productive? We could go downstairs to the gym and do some yoga," she prompted. "It might make you feel better and get you out of your funk."

"I don't have the energy to do much of anything right now." She'd kept mementoes of her time with Nico all over her room. Now everywhere she looked reminded her of him. The cocktail napkin from the W Hotel sat on her dresser, and a pair of pink fuzzy slippers he'd given to her sat beside her bed. A Founder's Day T-shirt and a goofy photo of the two of them in costume had been placed on a bookshelf. Little notes and cards were taped to her mirror. The roses from their first date were now tied with string and hanging upside down from her headboard. When she touched the edge of a petal, it fell like a tear.

"I'm here to listen if you want to talk," Arabella said in a soft voice.

Brooke looked over at Arabella and sighed. "He's gone for good." A part of her wondered if she'd ever get over this sense of loss, and another part of her would always be grateful for her time with Nico.

"You took a chance. But you can't give up. Nico's worth the fight." Arabella gave her an encouraging smile.

"It's too late." The pain in Brooke's chest expanded and threatened to crack open.

"It's never too late. You've waited your whole life to meet someone like Nico and now you've found the real deal."

"What if I'm stuck with Melinda's karma for the rest of my life?" Brooke's stomach knotted with nerves and misery.

"Wait a minute, Brooke, what about who you are in this life?" Arabella asked, scooting closer. "You're kind and giving to everyone. Doesn't that count for something? There has to be balance in the universe."

"Every part of me hopes you're right." Brooke's eyes stung with fresh tears. "I got closer and more emotionally invested in Nico than any other man in my life. Our souls are connected." They knew each other's deepest secrets and fears.

A loud clap of thunder made her jump, followed by a torrent of rain that pounded against the roof and shook the windows. Rivulets rushed down the side of the house like a waterfall. She hated storms.

"Everyone's headed downstairs to the basement to play board games over candlelight and eat cold leftovers in case the power goes out. You should join us," Arabella murmured in sympathy.

The howling of the wind whipping against the glass reminded Brooke of a wounded animal. Turning to the window, she stared at the dark, swirling clouds. "Don't you think it's a strange twist of fate that a nasty storm was brewing the night Melinda and Lucas tried to run away together?"

"Or some kind of divine providence."

Brooke's head snapped around. "Did you say providence?"

"Yeah, why?"

"*The Providence* was the name of the ship that was supposed to take Melinda and Lucas some place far away so they could get married." The second Brooke uttered the words, tingles shot up and down her arms. Familiarity clicked in her brain. A sense of *déjà vu* washed over her like a crashing wave. Jolting out of bed, she went to her desk, and grabbed her Ephemeris. She flipped through the pages until she found what she was looking for—tonight's position of the planets. "Venus will be transiting the Sun. The last time it made the journey was in September 1832, almost two hundred years ago, right after Melinda and Lucas perished and the curse was placed on my bloodline."

"Holy crap, there's no such thing as a cosmic coincidence." Arabella got up and met her at the desk.

"Maybe this isn't about using witchcraft or magick to break the curse, but more about clearing my karma. I have to go to the tree and ask for forgiveness for the sins of Melinda's past…my past, in order to clear it once and for all. What do you think?"

"I think you may be onto something." Arabella tapped her hand on the desk. "When I was twelve, I kept a diary and wrote a bunch of trash about these girls who were being mean to me. My mother read the diary and gave me a lecture on the power of my words. She insisted that I needed to clear my karma so that what I wrote didn't come back to me times three. I asked the goddess for forgiveness and burned the diary as a symbolic offering."

A flutter of excitement lifted her spirits. "What if I do the same with Melinda's and Lucas's love letters? I could burn them as a symbolic offering."

"Sounds like poetic justice to me."

"This means I have to go to the tree tonight." Brooke went to her closet and reached for her backpack off the hook.

"What? You can't go there tonight. Are you out of your effing mind? That's the worst place you can go during a storm." Arabella pointed to the window, where streaks of lightning lit up the sky. "You need to stay inside and hunker down."

"I've got to do this, Arabella, or I'll never be free. Neither will my children or their children if I stay in a relationship long enough to have any. If I don't do this, it will haunt me forever." Crossing the room to her nightstand, Brooke gathered up the letters from the top drawer and slipped them into her backpack.

"You could die out there. I get the Leo in you is courageous, but this is nuts. It's too dangerous." Arabella's voice rose. "You can't go out there alone."

"The way I see it, there's only one way to make things right. It's a chance I'm willing to take. Besides, Melinda will be looking out for me." She'd spent too many years thinking everything happened for a reason, but not anymore. Tonight, she'd turn the hand of fate. "I'm done looking over my shoulder, waiting for the other heel to drop. I have to fight for Nico…for us. The stakes have never been higher."

Arabella turned to another gust rattling the window. "At least wait until the storm blows over."

Taking several long, deep breaths, the implication sank in. "I can't. Nico and I have until midnight, or our love will be lost forever."

CHAPTER 15

NICO

*L*ast night, after Nico left Brooke's place, he went home and drank himself stupid, like some lovesick fool. Not one of his prouder moments. He woke up in a shitty mood with a vicious hangover.

He now stood in the hall of his uncle's house, where he'd spent the better part of an hour boxing up the coat closet. When his fingers closed over the brown fedora on the top shelf, he froze. His uncle had worn that hat everywhere. And then reality struck like a bolt of lightning. He'd never hear his laughter or see his smiling face ever again. Minutes ticked by. Not sure how long he stood there gripping the brim of the hat like a lifeline, instead of putting it in the box with the coats, he set the hat off to the side with a few other mementos that reminded him of the old man. Beating back the past, he sealed up the rest of the boxes, and tried like hell not to get swept up by grief. Getting the contents of the house ready for auction kept him from thinking about his breakup with Brooke, and right now he needed a distraction. He'd already rehashed the whole thing in his mind at least a dozen times and still came up short.

Alex came through the kitchen door holding a tape dispenser, shaking his head. "Talk about a pack rat. I just packed up everything in the cabinets and the drawers. The auctioneer's only interested in the furniture and the antiques, so we need to box up the rest of this stuff and get it out of here. The guy's going to have a field day with this place."

Glancing in the direction of the living room, Nico rubbed his chin. "I've been looking through some of his genealogy books and family trees. This stuff goes back generations. The extent of Uncle George's collection is insane." Knick-knacks, memorabilia, and stacks of old newspapers covered almost every available surface. "I'd say we have our work cut out for us."

A few hours later, they'd stacked up a wall of boxes in the family room. All that was left to go through were things of sentimental value and a cedar chest full of photo albums pulled from the attic.

Leaning back against the couch cushion, Nico flipped through the pages of black and white family photos, hoping to kill some time until the storm passed. "Some of these photos are hundreds of years old. I feel like I'm in a time warp." A wave of nostalgia settled over him. "I have no idea who half of these people are." He carefully pulled the photo out of the plastic and flipped it over so he could read the names on the back. "Whose Aunt Maria and Uncle Kostas?"

"No idea. What about Grandpa Dimitri and Grandma Sophia?" Alex asked from the wing back chair across from him. Several albums sat in front of his brother on the coffee table, along with a bottle of beer. "The guy sure liked to hold onto memories."

"No shit." Gusts of wind and pounding rain shook the old house on its hinges, drawing Nico's gaze to the wall of windows. Swallowing the lump now lodged in his throat, he hoped Brooke was somewhere dry and safe. He wanted to be there for her, to comfort her through the good times and the bad, and muddle through the storms together. But she'd cut him off at the knees.

"You okay?" Alex's voice drew him back to the conversation. "Are you thinking about Brooke? It's hard to believe you two are over."

The churning in Nico's gut returned. He turned back to face his brother and exhaled a frustrated breath. "She ended things. The ball's in her court now." Saying the words out loud burned his throat like acid.

"Shit, I'm sorry, Nico." Alex lifted his beer and took a sip. "You guys seemed great together. I could tell you were really into each other."

"We are...I mean we were," Nico amended, not able to stop the longing that hit him in the chest. "I could talk to her for hours and never get bored.

At the end of the day, she's the one person I want to say goodnight to and wake up to in the morning. She's it for me."

"I get it, dude. That's how I feel about Willow."

"From the first moment I saw Brooke, I knew I had to have her. She's sweet and funny. She's got this huge heart. There's this energy between us that I can't define." Nico's mouth went dry. "And the sex...hell, it's out of this fucking world."

Alex held up the neck of his bottle. "Whoa, TMI, but I suspected as much. That kind of chemistry is hard to find. I hope you two can patch things up."

"Yeah, well, it doesn't matter now. We're over." Nico gripped the couch pillow hard. "Can we talk about something else?"

"Sure, but I'm betting she'll come around." Alex set his bottle down and resumed sifting through the albums. Several minutes ticked by with neither of them saying a word, sitting in comfortable silence. "Holy shit, you've got to see this guy. Talk about a family resemblance! He could be your twin, Nico."

"What? Let me see." Anticipation coursed through Nico's veins as he got up from the couch and came up behind Alex to glance at the photo over his shoulder. He stared, speechless. The resemblance was uncanny. It was like looking at his mirror image. His hand shook a little as he reached for the photo. Nico's finger skimmed over the faded, worn edges and a flash of images rushed through his head like a movie in slow motion. When he turned the photo over, he noticed the date written in the corner, 7-7-1832, next to the name Lucas Denopoulos.

Shock gripped him by the throat. "Lucas," he murmured and froze. Could Nico be Lucas's reincarnated soul? If he was, then that meant Brooke's tale of love and loss wasn't some legend after all. Fuck, maybe the curse was real. "I've got to go."

"You look like you've seen a ghost. What the hell's going on?" Alex prompted, looking up at him, his brows drawn together. "Care to fill me in?"

"Not now." Pulling out his phone from his pocket, Nico pressed a button and prayed Brooke answered. No surprise, the call went straight to voicemail. "Dammit, she never answers her phone." Nico cursed as he waited for the beep. "Please call me the second you get this." After he ended the call, he glanced over at Alex. "I've got to get over to the manor. I need to talk to Brooke."

"Aren't you getting the alerts on your phone? Power lines are down and there's major flooding everywhere. Roads will be closed. Brooke will still be there when this storm blows over."

"You don't understand. This can't wait." His heart hammered in his chest like a jackknife.

His brother must've seen the desperation on his face. "I'll try Willow and see if she can get a hold of one of the witches." Alex grabbed his phone off the table and hopped off the couch. "I'll be right back."

Nico couldn't stay put, so he went to the closet, pulled on his rain slicker, and grabbed a flashlight off a shelf. Reaching for an umbrella from the stand, he turned at the sound of Alex's footsteps.

His brother frowned and held up his phone. "I'm sorry to be the one to tell you this, but Brooke's out there in the storm."

The room spun. "What are you talking about?" She'd mentioned her fear of storms. She'd never go out in this. Nico's pulse spiked with adrenaline.

"She went to Elysian Park, something about burning letters at some tree. I don't understand. Why would Brooke go there alone in the middle of a storm?"

The question hit Nico in the gut. *Why indeed.* "I'm sorry. There's no time to explain."

"You'll never make it in your Mustang. Take my truck and then come back and get me." Reaching into his pocket, Alex threw him his keys. "I'll send you a map of the open roads so you can get their faster. Be careful."

Panic sliced through him when he thought about Brooke out there in the storm alone. *I pray I'm not too late.*

CHAPTER 16

BROOKE

The drive to the park took Brooke hours. She navigated her Beetle through roads without working traffic lights and multiple detours. She'd somehow managed to avoid downed wires and flooding that would have reached the top of her hood.

Her wiper blades squeaked as rain splashed against the windshield. Streaks of lightning lit up the dark sky. When she finally came to the park entrance, she swore her car floated into a spot.

After she cut the engine, she pulled her backpack off the seat and slung it over her shoulder. Lifting the hood on her raincoat, she offered a silent prayer to the goddess to keep her safe. She could do this. She had no choice.

Her breaths grew shallow, and her heart pounded against her ribcage. She gave herself a mental pep talk and reached for the door handle. The second she got out of the car, the icy spray of rain soaked her straight to the bone. Pounding rain echoed in the open field. She pulled out her flashlight and clicked it on, maneuvering over branches and upturned tree roots, trudging through the grass, soaking wet and shaking.

Her boots made a swishing sound as she sloshed through giant puddles. A gust of torrential wind smacked her in the face, and the dread in her stomach returned full throttle. When she imagined her life without

Nico, a stabbing pain pierced her heart. She'd always dreamed of a partner molded from the heavens, created by the gods themselves. Nico surpassed every one of her wildest fantasies. She refused to accept that their relationship was broken beyond repair.

Once Brooke made it to the tree, she shined the light on the initials carved into the bark. A part of her wanted to sink to the ground and bury her face in her hands and sob, but it wouldn't do her any good. She needed to be strong and kick this curse's ass, end this thing once and for all. Whatever cosmic forces that may be at work needed to play out tonight

She intended to wage a war against Mother Nature and the hand of fate, and prayed she'd be the one to come out on top. The roar of thunder seemed to amplify her conviction. Pulling out the letters from her backpack, she turned and glanced at the tree, shaking from head to toe.

"Please forgive me for what I did in a past life. Accept these letters as an offering, a symbol of my desire to break this curse and clear my karma, so I can set things right."

Reaching inside the pocket of her rain slicker, her wet fingers closed over the lighter she'd slipped inside. When she tried to light the letters, the flame kept blowing out from the wind and rain. After several tries, she finally got the edge of the paper to light and then shielded the letters from the rain until they burned to ash, dropping them just before they could scorch her fingers. The wind whipped up the ashes floating through the air, sending them in every direction.

"Goodbye, Melinda. I'm using this as a symbolic offering for payment rendered. All I want is to break this curse for me and my future generations. Please, I can't live this way anymore." Brooke repeated the words until her soul cried out. When she thought about losing Nico forever, her world threatened to collapse into a pit of darkness.

Her heart felt like it might split in two and break apart. She closed her eyes and willed her mind to focus on happy memories with Nico, concentrating on every blissful detail.

"Come with me, my love and stay forever and a day," she whispered the words over and over again. And then she heard her name on the wind. She figured she must be hallucinating.

"Brooke?" The voice called out again

This time the voice grew louder and more distinct. She turned and stared in the distance, her mouth falling open on a gasp. Nico ran toward her, sloshing over deep puddles. The sight of him stirred a deep yearning. Hope warmed her insides and almost made her forget about the chill.

"What are you doing here? How did you find me?"

"Do you think I'd leave you out here alone? I don't want to lose you." Nico grabbed her by the shoulders and squeezed. Rain poured from his lashes and pooled at his lip. His clothes were plastered to his large frame. "I told you, we're in this together."

Happy tears stung her eyes. "You do realize that the Aries in you has a knight in shining armor complex?" Some of the pain lifted from her heart.

"Maybe. I'm sorry for not believing you about the curse." He wrapped his arms around her shivering body. "I saw a photo of Lucas at my uncle's house. He's my ancestor, Brooke."

A chill that had zero to do with the rain slid down her spine. "It makes perfect sense."

"You need to talk to me when things get rough. I can't take it when you pull away from me."

"I tried to tell you, Nico—"

Regret burned in his eyes. "You're right, and I wouldn't listen. I'm an ass." His fingers touched her wet lips. "After I told you about my divorce, you asked me what brought back my faith in humanity and allowed me to trust again. It was my hope of opening my restaurant and following my dream, but it was also putting my trust in people again, and the one person I've put all of my trust in is you."

Her heart turned over. "You're such a romantic. It's one of the many things I love about you."

"Whoa, what did you say? Did I hear you right?" Tilting her chin up, a wide smile played across his lips.

Tears welled in her eyes. "The only thing I can think of to break the curse is to declare our love, here at the tree." The truth of her words tore through her with the force of the gusting wind. "The answer's been inside me all along."

Nico bent his head and sealed his lips over hers in a blistering kiss that stole her breath. His tongue flicked into her mouth and danced with hers in lush, hot sweeps. She tasted her future...her forever. Brooke reached up on her tiptoes and wound her arms around his neck, digging her fingers into his wet hair to bring him closer. His erection pressed against her thigh and a deep longing spread to every part of her body. Tears poured from her eyes and mixed with the rain. The idea of never having Nico again left her shaking. The storm continued to unfold around them, but nothing else seemed to matter.

Tilting her chin up, his tongue plunged deeper. She moaned into his mouth and flicked against it with deep strokes of her own. And then her mind hazed with need, thinking she'd never get the chance to taste the man she loved again.

The kiss raged on like the storm. Nico's lips never left hers, not even to draw in breath, as though he feared breaking the kiss might end things forever.

Brooke pulled back, breathless. "I love you, Nico Denopoulos, with all my heart and soul. I love your humor and your creativity. I love your kisses and your passion for life. I love the way you make me feel when I'm with you. I've never known real love before you. I've always been afraid to lay my heart on the line, but not anymore. You're my forever."

Cupping her face in his hands, Nico brushed his thumb over her wet cheek. "I love you, Brooke Howe, with all my heart, and with each day my love has grown and blossomed bigger than this damn tree. I love that you're kind and courageous. I love the sound of your laugh. You've made me better in every way possible. You see me for who I am. You understand me in a way that no one else ever has. What I feel for you…hell, it's all consuming. I tried to find someone I could spend my life with and that someone is you. I love you with every breath in my body. You're my soulmate." A bolt of lightning lit up the sky, right next to the tree like a sign from above.

"Nico…" Brooke surrendered to the power of his words.

"No curse will ever have the power to make me forget you," he murmured. "You're woven into my soul."

More tears ran down her cheeks at his beautiful words. "I love you." Through the corner of her eye, Brooke caught a glimpse of a blue light circling around them. The light grew brighter then shot into the sky. "Something's happening."

"What's going on?" He pointed to the blue light flickering above their heads. "It's like the Northern Lights, right here in Raven's Hollow."

Fluffy, white clouds floated above them. Brooke's mouth fell open when two shadowy figures dressed in nineteenth century clothing appeared. She recognized Melinda, and the stunning man beside her looked exactly like Nico. He had to be Lucas. They ran to each other and kissed, and then the clouds floated away, turning into two giant blue orbs.

"Holy shit! Did you see that?"

Brooke laughed and cried at the same time. "I'm free. The curse is broken."

The rain stopped and the wind died down. They belonged together, and the stars agreed.

"I love you, Brooke, and I'll never stop. I want to wake up next to you every day. What do you say, will you move in with me?"

"I say yes! I'm yours, Nico, yours forever."

Thank you for reading! Did you enjoy? Please add your review because nothing helps an author more and encourages readers to take a chance on a book than a review.

And don't miss more from Shari Nichols coming soon!

Until then read <u>EDGE OF THE WOODS</u>, by City Owl Author, Jules Kelley.
Turn the page for a sneak peek!

Also be sure to sign up for the City Owl Press newsletter to receive notice of all book releases!

SNEAK PEEK OF EDGE OF THE WOODS

BY JULES KELLEY

The sun crested the horizon, lighting the inside of the truck with an orange glow, and Leland stretched, trying to work eighteen hours of road stiffness out of his shoulders. In the distance, mountains rose above the scraggly pines like towering angels against the brightening sky, welcoming him to paradise instead of throwing him out. He spared one hand off the steering wheel to knuckle the dust and sleepless itch out of his eyes and wished for another cup of coffee.

Taking the job in Pine Grove had been a risk, but as far as he was concerned, it was already paying off. He'd washed off the last of the dust from the Arizona desert at a gas station somewhere north of Salt Lake City, and now, watching the foothills of western Montana fill his view, he barely remembered what Tucson looked like.

When he'd interviewed with the Upham County Sheriff's Department, Sheriff Rylan had told him that Pine Grove was the basement office of deputy assignments.

"'Bout once a month, you'll have to go out on the nature preserve to find some birdbrain out-of-towner who got lost on the full moon. The town trades on old folktales 'bout werewolves in the woods, and some people are dumb enough to go lookin'. Other than that, hope you like sittin' around with your thumb up your ass waitin' for somebody to lock themselves out of their house."

That sounded just fine to Leland. Hell, he might even have time to go fishing every now and then. The fancy fly rod he'd bought himself a couple of years ago hadn't been doing anything except collecting dust in his closet, and the Tucson PD staff therapist had brought it up in his final session.

"When's the last time you took some time off to just enjoy a hobby?"

Well, no time like the present.

A flash of movement on the side of the road caught his attention—an animal stumbling up out of the ditch right in front of him—and he swore as he stomped on the brakes, pulling hard on the steering wheel. His heartbeat thudded in his ears as the vehicle skidded sideways, tires squawking as they jumped and bounced over the asphalt. The SUV finally came to a stop with one tire in the ditch, and he pried his shaking hands off the steering wheel to scrape them over his face.

He turned to look at the animal he'd almost hit and sucked in a sharp breath when he realized it wasn't a bear or a deer, but a human, naked and filthy, hunched over as he lurched unsteadily across the pavement.

Leland was out of the driver's seat in an instant, automatically reaching for his handset to radio Guerrera, and then swore when he remembered. He wasn't in uniform. He wasn't in Arizona. Guerrera was twelve hundred miles away. He wasn't even a police officer anymore. He patted his pockets instead, looking for his phone and digging it out as he cautiously approached the man.

Boy, he corrected himself as he got closer. It was hard to tell what his face looked like under streaks of dirt—*And is that dried blood?*—but he was small, slender, his dark eyes large in his ashy brown face. Late teens, Leland guessed, forcing down the itch of memory at the back of his mind: another young face, another pair of haunted eyes. He didn't have time for that right now.

"Hey," Leland called, one hand out to him, moving slowly. "Are you all right, kid?"

The boy didn't answer him, but he watched Leland warily. He drew in several quick breaths through his nose, and after a moment, Leland realized he was sniffing the air. His mannerisms were more animal than human, but his hair was shaved close on the sides, a stylish—and recent—haircut, and a diamond earring glinted from the dirt caking his right ear, so he hadn't been out of civilization that long.

"It's all right. I'm here to help you," Leland tried again, keeping his voice calm and quiet. He thought of the legends of werewolves in Pine Grove that Rylan had told him about and just as quickly shook off the idea.

The boy, naked and bloody, had clearly been through *something*, but Leland knew intimately that run-of-the-mill humans were more than capable of incredible cruelty without any supernatural assistance.

"Can you tell me your name?" Leland said, trying to keep the boy's attention as he inched back toward his SUV. Somewhere in the meager life's belongings in the back seat of the vehicle were clothes that might fit the kid, at least enough to cover him up and keep him from freezing. The day was rapidly warming as the sun rose, but spring nights in Montana were still chilly, and he'd obviously been out for at least a few hours.

Leland checked his phone as he sifted through one of his duffel bags. One bar of signal. Maybe it would be enough to call somebody, see if he could get an ambulance on the way. He only had two local numbers—the Upham County sheriff's office and the Pine Grove Wildlife Preserve. The sheriff's office was in Red Horse River, another hour and a half up the road, and Rylan *had* said that the preserve director would be his point of contact for problems with wayward tourists, lost hikers, and animal attacks.

Well, here goes nothin'.

He tucked the phone between his ear and shoulder, listening to it ring as he finally found a pair of sweat pants that looked like they might fit the kid if he pulled the drawstring tight.

There was a click, then silence, and Leland waited to hear someone on the other end. "Hello?" Nothing. "Hello, can you hear me?"

The beep of a dropped call mocked him, and he huffed out a frustrated breath. "Dammit."

The young man twitched, seeming to focus on him for the first time, his gaze confused and curious—but finally human, not glassy and alien.

"Who're you?"

"Hey, kid," Leland said, immediately pocketing his phone again. "My name's Leland Sommers. I found you out here on the road. You remember how you got here?"

The kid looked around, frowning, and Leland guessed the answer before he shook his head. "Where the fuck is *here*?"

He shivered, and Leland held out the sweat pants in offering. The kid's nose wrinkled, but he took them.

"You're on Route 23, right outside Pine Grove, Montana." He cleared his throat. "What's your name?" He focused on keeping his voice steady and warm. The boy didn't seem especially volatile, but neither had that one girl he'd found stoned out of her mind on the floor of her boyfriend's meth lab—until she'd damn near taken a chunk out of his arm.

This guy looked more like something had already taken a bite out of *him*, Leland thought, eyeing a fresh-looking wound on the kid's left shoulder.

"My name's Diego." Diego wet his lips, pulling the drawstring on the pants as tight as they would go. They still sagged on his narrow hips, the *Arizona Coyotes* logo down the leg looking bigger than his entire body.

Leland's phone rang in his pocket, and Diego flinched and immediately looked around as if he'd lost something, swearing under his breath. Leland guessed he'd had a phone with him before whatever had happened. But he'd have to ask questions later; the call was coming from a local number.

"This is Leland Sommers."

"You call this number a minute ago?" The woman's voice on the other end of the line was brusque, no-nonsense. "This is the Pine Grove Nature Preserve's ranger station."

"I did." Well, at least something was going right. "I'm the new sheriff's deputy, coming to fill the position in town. I'm stopped on Route 23 out here east of town with a young man who was in the road with no clothes on. Is there an emergency response service that I should call?"

The woman on the other end made a noise that might have been a snort. "Closest hospital's at least an hour away. Can you get him into your car and drive him in, or do you need a backboard and a neck brace?"

Leland darted a glance over at Diego, evaluating him. He was trying to pick the leaves and twigs out of his hair now; it didn't seem at all like he was nursing a spinal injury.

"No, he's ambulatory." Diego gave him an odd look, frowning, and Leland had a sudden flash of another kid—younger, smaller, but with the same mix of wariness and cautious hope on his face. He looked away. "Where should I take him?"

"There's a clinic. When you're coming in to town, turn left at the stoplight, and you'll see it in about half a mile. I'll call Haley and Doc Fenton, let 'em know you're comin' in."

"Which stoplight?" Leland asked, and the woman laughed.

"The only one in the whole town. Anything you want me to tell the doc when I call her? Injuries, things like that?"

"Just some contusions, abrasions. It does look like he got attacked by an animal, maybe. Large wound on his shoulder might be a bite mark."

The woman went so quiet that Leland pulled the phone away from his ear to see if the call had dropped.

"Hello?"

"I'll let them know," she said and hung up without a good-bye.

The clinic had a single lightbulb above the door, glowing brightly in the misty morning, and one lonely car parked in the parking lot.

Diego was shivering by the time Leland helped him down from the passenger's seat, teeth chattering, little muscle spasms shooting through him.

"You're gonna be all right," Leland murmured, supporting him carefully, noting the feverish heat in his skin. A peek at Diego's face confirmed that his eyes had gone glassy again, little beads of sweat at his hairline. "We're here at the clinic. We're gonna get you taken care of."

The door was locked, and Leland pressed the button labeled FOR SERVICE AFTER HOURS. Within seconds, a woman in jeans and flannel with short-cropped gray hair unlocked the door and pushed it open with an urgency that Leland appreciated.

"You're the one that called in to the preserve?" the woman said, already reaching for Diego, gloved hand brushing his hair out of his face to look at his eyes.

"Yeah." Leland lifted Diego over the threshold when the kid couldn't seem to pick his feet up enough to get past the doorstep. "You the doctor?"

"I'm Dr. Fenton." She locked the door behind them and led them through the empty lobby, the fluorescent lights flickering and buzzing to life when she flicked the switch. "Can you help me get him to the exam room?"

"Nice to meet you, Doc." Leland grunted at the unexpected weight as Diego went almost limp against him, and he hitched his arm more securely around Diego's middle. "I'm Leland." As an afterthought, he added, "His name's Diego."

She swept ahead of them into an exam room and helped Leland get Diego up onto the patient table, the white paper crinkling loudly.

A buzzer sounded, and Diego groaned, covering his ears.

"That'll be Haley," Dr. Fenton said, changing out her gloves for fresh ones. "The preserve director. Do you mind letting her in for me?"

"Yeah, I got it." Leland steadied Diego before finding his way back through the clinic toward the front door. When he first saw the girl standing on the other side of the glass, he wondered if maybe it was someone's daughter instead of Haley Fern, Director of the Pine Grove Nature Preserve. Nothing about her, from her blond ponytail to the soft roundness of her face and generous curves of her figure, matched the gruff, no-nonsense voice he'd heard on the phone that morning. Then again, she was clutching a travel mug with LUANN'S DINER emblazoned on the side like it was the only thing keeping her standing, so maybe that was just how she sounded when she got dragged out of bed at the crack of dawn on a Saturday morning.

When he approached the door, she lifted the huge sunglasses that had been covering half her face, and wow, those big, brown eyes could stop a full-grown man in his tracks. They almost did.

He fumbled the door open a crack and leaned out a bit, staying cautious in case he was wrong. He'd been wrong before. "Can I help you?"

She squinted up at him, her nose wrinkling under a dusting of dark freckles. Christ, she was so cute it was almost illegal.

"I'm Haley Fern, the preserve director," she said, and he knew immediately it wasn't the same person he'd talked to that morning. Her voice was too sweet for that. "And you are?"

He had the oddest impulse to take his cap off, but he just held the door open wider for her instead. "Leland Sommers, the new dedicated deputy. I called the preserve this morning about a kid I found on the way in. That wasn't you I talked to, was it?"

"Oh, no, that was my ranger, Michele." She ducked in under his arm as he held open the door, still eyeing him like she was sizing him up. "You're the one they hired to take George's place? We weren't expecting you until tomorrow night."

She was half his height, but he felt almost scolded. It was all he could do not to feel like he was telling his teacher why he didn't have his homework. "My lease was already up at my old place, so I figured I'd come up a couple days early, start getting settled in."

He locked the door behind her, and when he turned around, she was rubbing one eye and biting back a yawn. No one had a right to be that cute and that intimidating at the same time.

She caught him watching her and waved one hand apologetically. "Sorry. Not a morning person. Michele said the boy you found was injured?"

He nodded, shortening his stride so he could walk beside her down the hall. "Bite marks. Looked like maybe a dog or coyote from glancing at it. 'Bout the right size and depth, compared to other likely things." At her sideways glance, he shrugged, guessing at her unasked question. "Saw a few animal attacks on the force in Arizona."

He shut his mouth, clenching his jaw against the echo of snarls and growls that were even louder than the screams…

Haley pushed the door to the exam room open, and Leland was grateful for the opportunity to focus on something else. Diego sat on the bench, his knuckles almost white where his fingers were curled around the edge, his jaw clenched so hard the tendons were standing out in his neck.

"Diego, this is my friend Haley," Dr. Fenton said. "She'd like to talk to you about what happened last night, if that's okay."

Leland was several feet away, but he could still hear Diego's breathing go ragged, the whites of his eyes visible as he started shivering.

"You don't have to," Haley said quickly as Diego swayed, and Leland stepped forward, bracing Diego gingerly by his upper arms. The boy twitched at his touch, but his skin was clammy and cold underneath a thin layer of sweat. "Karen, I think he's…"

Dr. Fenton nodded, opening a drawer and pulling out a plastic-wrapped syringe.

"Can you breathe for me, Diego?" she said calmly as she pulled the wrapper apart. "Your heart is beating very quickly, so I'm going to give you something to relax you, but can you help me by focusing on your breathing? Breathe in…and out. In…and out." She kept up the soothing breath count while she plunged the needle into a bottle, pulling the clear liquid up into the syringe. "That's it. You're doing great."

Diego flinched when he saw the needle, but when he pressed backward, Leland was there, blocking his route. Dr. Fenton kept talking to him in a calm, soothing voice as she slid the needle into his arm, and within seconds, Leland felt Diego relaxing, starting to slump over.

He lowered the boy to the padded bench, moving out of the way when Haley appeared with a soft blanket that she wrapped around Diego's torso, tucking it under him gently. She didn't seem to notice Leland watching her as she leaned forward to look at the bite mark on Diego's shoulder, and…was she…sniffing him? Maybe to see if he smelled like alcohol, but Leland hadn't noticed any indication that the kid might have been drinking.

"I appreciate your help, Deputy Sommers," Dr. Fenton said, drawing his attention. "He's lucky you found him when you did."

Seems like it would've been luckier if someone had found him earlier, Leland thought, but he just nodded. "Glad to help," he said instead. "Sorry to ask, but do you have a restroom I could use?"

"Of course. Down the hall on the right."

He thanked her and headed toward the door she'd indicated, trying not to hurry too obviously. Now that the immediate crisis was over, his body was reminding him that he was only human, and he'd had approximately a gallon of coffee since he'd left Arizona.

As he washed his hands afterward, he caught sight of his reflection in the mirror and grimaced. It was a damn wonder not one of the three people he'd seen that morning had run screaming, what with the bloodshot eyes, two days' worth of stubble, and messy hair curling up from under his baseball cap. Then again, all three of them had bigger things to worry about. But so much for first impressions as the new deputy, he thought, scrubbing a hand over his whiskery jaw. Maybe Haley and the doc wouldn't hold it against him.

And maybe one of them could point him toward the best place to get another round of coffee to keep him on his feet until he could at least get his meager belongings out of the truck and into the new place. Maybe some breakfast too. He thought of the sticker on Haley's thermos and headed back down the hallway, intent on asking her for directions.

The door to the exam room was cracked open, and he could see the two women talking with their heads bent close together, though they stopped and looked up as soon as they heard his footsteps. It made him feel a little put on the spot, especially the way Dr. Fenton pressed her fingertips to her mouth like she was hoping he hadn't heard what she'd been saying.

"Sorry to interrupt," he said, trying for his best friendly smile now that he knew what a mess they were looking at. He wouldn't blame them if they'd been discussing him; he'd think twice about trusting the man he'd seen in the mirror too. "I was wonderin' if you could point me toward someplace to get some coffee and a bite to eat."

Haley's expression shifted from cautious to cheerful in the space it took her to blink. "I'll do you one better," she said. "I can't ask Diego any questions until he wakes up, and Karen says he needs to rest for a while, so why don't I just take you?"

The parking lot at Luann's was about half full, probably peak breakfast crowd, and Haley wrinkled her nose. A good half her pack was here, and if there was one thing she knew about small-town werewolves, it was that they stuck their noses into everyone else's business, especially hers. All part of being the alpha, her mother used to say.

But Haley couldn't imagine anyone sticking their nose in her mother's business and living to tell about it, so maybe it was just all part of her whole pack having known her since she was knee-high. Either way, they were all going to be extremely interested in the new deputy and in why Haley was out and about before ten a.m. on a Saturday, and she'd rather keep both things to herself for now.

Especially the new deputy, she thought as she watched him ease his Chevy Blazer into the gravel spot next to hers, his dusty Arizona plates catching the sunlight. Maybe it was because she'd broken up with her boyfriend before she left Seattle and hadn't been seeing anyone else in the nine months she'd been back in town, or maybe it was because the full moon was only three days away and making her antsy, but she was a little ticked off about how good-looking he was, especially when she knew she couldn't do anything about it.

"Welcome to Pine Grove, Deputy," she called as he opened his door and stepped out, moving stiffly. She guessed the long drive was starting to catch up with him. God knew that after the last time she'd driven back from Seattle, she'd shifted into a wolf and gone for a run just to stretch her legs as soon as she'd gotten home.

"Just Leland is fine," he said, removing his cap long enough to rake his hair away from his face before he settled it back on his head. "Hell of a welcome wagon you rolled out there." His smile was the barest quirk of his lips, and it did awful, terrible things to her pulse. *Dang.*

"Oh, we throw wounded kids at every new deputy that comes to town," she joked with a grimace. "He didn't tell you where he was from or anything like that, did he?"

He shook his head, and she wondered if it was bad to feel such a wash of relief. Notifying family members would have to wait until they could confirm whether that bite on Diego's shoulder had done what she thought it had, so she was glad she didn't have to make excuses for why she was putting it off.

"Nah, he didn't talk much. Barely got his name out of him. Figure it was the shock."

The bell over the door jangled as she pulled it open, and the smell of sizzling bacon hit her straight in the nose, drawing an audible growl from her stomach. She sensed the ripple of movement through the dining room as they came in, the curiosity of twenty werewolves and their family members at the sight of a new person in town.

"Haley Fern, what are you doin' out so early on your day off?" Sally called from where she was pulling down orders from the kitchen window. "And—oh, who's your friend?"

Well, whoever hadn't noticed them before sure as heck had now.

"Sally, this is Leland Sommers. He's the new deputy, just got in this morning. Leland, this is Sally Newcrow. She and her sister, Luann, own the diner."

"Nice to meet you." Leland nodded politely. "Sure does smell good in here."

"Tastes good too." Sally grinned at him as she loaded her arms up with plates of food to take out to the tables. "Well, sit your butts down, and I'll get to you in a second."

Haley led him over to the last empty booth, hoping the high benches would give them some semblance of privacy, and pulled the laminated, handwritten menus out of the holder, handing one to him as he got settled.

"You can't go wrong with anything here," she promised, looking at the menu to keep from staring at him, even though the offerings hadn't changed in twenty years and Haley always got the exact same thing.

Behind Leland, Sally caught her eye and mouthed, *He is so hot!* It took all Haley's self-control not to roll her eyes. Sally pulled her pencil out of her ponytail and flipped to a new page on her notepad as she sidled up to their table.

"It sure is exciting to get to meet the new deputy," she said brightly. "We ain't had anyone new in town since Jo Pham managed to convince Brooks Carmody to move in with her back when Haley's momma was still—"

"Sally," Haley interrupted before Sally could get off track and blurt out incriminating details. "I'm sure he'd rather order his food."

Sally giggled, waving her hand. "Oh, don't mind me, Deputy. What're you havin' to eat?"

He flipped the menu over, still scanning the list of items. "Uh, Miss Fern says I can't go wrong with anything here…"

Sally mouthed *Miss Fern!* at her over his head, and this time Haley did roll her eyes.

"So how about the pancakes and bacon?"

"You got it, sugar. And Haley's right—everything here's the best you ever had, includin' your momma's cookin'."

Leland snorted, tucking his menu back into the holder. "Well, that wouldn't be a hard standard to beat." There was a faint tension at the corners of his mouth when he said it that made Haley think there might be a story there, and she didn't realize where Sally was headed with her train of thought until it was too late.

"Well, at least that means your future wife won't be intimidated in the kitchen," Sally said cheerfully, and Haley gave her a horrified look that she didn't bother hiding from Leland. "Or are you already married, Deputy?"

"Give me the steak and eggs, Sally," Haley blurted, talking over her, desperate to stop the impending disaster of a conversation. "And coffee."

"Uh, no, I'm not married." Amusement sparkled in his eyes as he folded his hands on the table, glancing at Haley, and she wanted to slide right off the bench. "And I'll have a coffee too, please. Black."

"Comin' right up, sugar. Y'all just hang tight."

Haley shook her head as Sally walked off to put their orders in, embarrassed laughter bubbling up in her throat. "Sorry about that. It's a small town, and like she said, we don't get new residents often. People get nosy. You can tell 'em to buzz off, I promise."

Leland chuckled, leaning back in the booth. "It's all right. Small towns are like that. At least so far everybody's been friendly, not like where I grew up."

"Arizona?" Haley guessed, but he shook his head.

"Nah, Idaho."

She waited, but he didn't expand on that. "That's not too far away from here."

Sally dropped off their cups of coffee, black for Leland and with a pitcher of cream for Haley, and he hummed, noncommittal, as he picked his up and took a sip. Haley poured the whole little pitcher into hers until it turned light tan and added two packs of sugar. He didn't seem interested in talking about Idaho, and despite her rampant curiosity, she decided it would be rude to pry.

"Are you staying here in town?" she asked instead. There wasn't much in the way of lodging for visitors, just the twenty-two rooms at the Sundown Motel, the seven empty RV spots at the Timber Trails Trailer Park, and the three suites at the Carmody Bed & Breakfast. "Or did you get a place in Red Horse River?"

The county seat was where most of the rest of the sheriff department employees lived, although it wasn't a metropolis itself, by any means.

"I'm renting an apartment here, but I don't know if it's ready yet." He smiled, rolling his coffee cup between his palms. It was already half empty, Haley noticed. "I wasn't supposed to be here until tomorrow night, so I might have to get a room somewhere."

Haley blinked. "An apartment?" In Pine Grove? She couldn't think of a single place. Maybe someone was renting him a room in their house, in which case she was a little peeved that no one had told her that option was on the table. She had an empty room at her place—not that having him underfoot all the time would be a great idea. She kept catching a whiff of him on her inhales, underneath the coffee and breakfast scents of the diner. The full moon being so close meant that the wolf was right at the surface of her consciousness, harder to ignore than usual, and the wolf thought Leland smelled *delicious*.

Down, girl.

"Yeah, it's a room over the newspaper office, I think she said? The woman I talked to said it hadn't been lived in for a while." He took a sip of his coffee, watching her over the edge of the cup like he was hoping she'd have a clue what he was talking about.

"Oh!" She'd forgotten Jo used to put out a community newsletter before she'd gotten too busy with the bed-and-breakfast and then having a baby. There was a one-bedroom apartment above the old printing office that they used for storage now, and Jo must have decided to clean it up and rent it out. "Yeah, Jo used to live there when she put out the *Howler*. I forgot about that."

"The *Howler*." Leland smirked. "Sheriff Rylan said you guys have some kind of werewolf thing going on for tourists. What's that about?"

Haley laughed nervously, clutching her coffee cup. Her mother had always said she was a *terrible* liar, but when your regional alpha said that the new deputy couldn't know anything about the pack of werewolves that made up most of the town's population…well, she'd give it her best shot.

"Yeah, the original town charter has all these provisions for werewolves and werewolf-human cooperation. Nobody's sure what the founders were thinking, but it gives us a nice little draw for tourist traffic. Gotta pay for the nature preserve somehow."

"It's not a federal or state preserve, then?" Leland looked mildly interested at that, fiddling with his coffee cup—empty already, Haley noticed.

"No, it's private land. One of the town founders owned it and designated it as a preserve about the same time they drew up the charter. It's officially owned by the town these days. There's a small American gray wolf family that lives there, so at least there actually *is* something for the tourists to look at, if they're lucky enough to get a glimpse."

Sally's sudden appearance with the coffeepot as soon as Leland drained his cup meant she was hovering close enough to eavesdrop, but Haley couldn't really fault her for that. The whole diner was probably listening, putting that wolf hearing to good use. The pack already knew that the new deputy wasn't being let in on the secret, but it didn't hurt for them to know what he'd been told. The last time an outsider had accidentally found out about the town's unusual demographics was still a cautionary tale passed down through generations, and nobody wanted a repeat of that mess.

"Do you think that might have been what attacked Diego?" Leland asked, and Sally almost dropped the coffeepot. So that news hadn't spread yet, then.

"I hope not," Haley said, ignoring Sally for the moment. "They've never shown aggression toward humans before. We get campers and hikers who try to break the rules and stay overnight in the preserve, but we don't see many animal attacks. A couple of boys got scared up a tree by a bear last year, but she just ate their food and trashed their campsite before she moved on."

Leland snorted. "Guess people are the same everywhere. Can't tell you how many of my calls in Tucson were to rescue people from something that never would have happened if they'd just paid attention to the safety regulations."

Haley relaxed a little, grateful that he hadn't pushed her on it. "Yeah, some people are convinced the rules are only there to spoil their fun. In our case, a lot of people think they're also there to keep the werewolves a secret." Which was true, but that didn't mean it wasn't also for safety purposes.

"So how long have you been the preserve director?" He held eye contact with her as he took a sip of his fresh coffee, and she was struck by how *blue* his eyes were, even bloodshot and tired.

"Almost a year." Her smile felt tight and tense even to her, and she tried to relax. "My mom was the preserve director before me. I always expected to take over from her—went to college in Seattle to get a master's in wildlife conservation, even—but I just didn't expect it to be *yet*." She laughed ruefully, rubbing at her forehead. "It's been…a lot."

"What happened?" There was a gentleness to his voice that caught her attention, made her notice the way he leaned in, his face open. "Is she…did she...?"

"Got married," Haley said flatly, amused by the flash of surprise in his expression. "She met a guy while I was in college, brought him to my graduation with her, and that's when she told me she was moving to Columbus, Ohio, with him."

"Damn. That must have been a surprise."

"You're tellin' me." She shrugged. "Nobody else in town wanted to take over, and everybody figured I was going to do it anyway, so here I am."

"Funny." Leland chuckled, but Sally appeared at the table with plates of food, cutting off whatever he'd been about to say.

They got the plates arranged, silverware rolled out, and after Leland had spread butter on his pancakes and started cutting them into pieces, she prompted him.

"Funny?"

"Oh, just..." He popped a giant pancake triangle into his mouth, no syrup, and chewed it thoughtfully. "Sheriff told me nobody wanted the deputy job. You got yours because nobody else wanted it." He shrugged. "Funny coincidence is all."

Haley laughed, cutting into her steak, her mouth watering at the deep-red color inside. *Perfect.* "Well, when you go into town to do your paper work and orientation, you'll find out why nobody wanted the deputy position. This place has a *reputation.*"

"Oh yeah?" Leland grinned at her, seeming more relaxed by the moment, and she felt some of the stark loneliness of the past nine months ease away, like a weight lifting. "What, because of the werewolf thing?"

Haley nodded. "That, and by extension, the tourists. You really will have more work to do around the full moon."

"That's all right. Just promise me there's no Bigfoot to contend with, and I'll cope with the werewolves." The glint of mischief in his eyes belied his dry tone, and Haley's heart skipped a beat. *Dang it, he's cute.*

"No Bigfoot that I know of," she promised, holding up three fingers like a Girl Scout.

He laughed, breaking off a piece of bacon and stuffing it into his mouth. "Well, you're the first person I'm calling if I find him."

Was he flirting? *Don't I wish.*

"That's fair." She shoved a bite of steak into her mouth and immediately lost her train of thought, salt and blood flooding across her tongue and soothing the constant itch of hunger at the back of her mind. She groaned, her eyes slipping closed, and let herself get lost in the taste for a moment. When she opened her eyes again, it was to see Leland watching her, one corner of his mouth pulled up in a crooked smile, and she blushed.

"Sorry," she muttered, laughing, and covered her mouth as she swallowed. "I'm really hungry."

"No apology necessary," Leland assured her, and she wondered if she was imagining the extra rasp to his voice. She didn't have much time to think about it, though, as her phone vibrated in her back pocket, buzzing loudly against the booth seat, the sound nearly making her jump out of her skin.

A glance at the screen showed that the call was coming from the clinic, and she put her fork down and sat back from the table a bit.

"Sorry," she told Leland. "I need to take this." She didn't wait for his nod to accept the call. "Hey, what's up?"

There was a clatter in the background, and then Karen said, "Haley, I'm so sorry. I know you just left, but I need you to stop back by. The sooner the better."

Haley's heart dropped into her stomach. "Of course. I'll be there in just a minute." She hung up and gave Leland an apologetic smile. "Sorry to run out on you. Do you need directions to your apartment, or do you know where you're going?"

"I can figure it out," he said, polite, giving her an easy smile. "Thanks, though."

Sally appeared with a to-go box, confirming Haley's suspicion that she was still eavesdropping, but Haley couldn't bring herself to care. She packed up the steak and bacon, pushing the plate with the eggs on it over toward Leland.

"Here, as my apology for ditching you. Plus, they won't reheat very well."

"I won't let 'em go to waste," he promised, and she grabbed her box, headed to the register to pay.

"Put his bill with mine," she told Sally quietly. "Welcome-to-town breakfast and all."

"Uh-huh." Sally grinned at her as she rang up both meals and waited for Haley to count out the cash for the total. "I'd like to eat *him* for breakfast."

"*Shh!*" Haley hissed, glancing toward the booth. She could barely see the back of Leland's head over the high back of the bench, his blue baseball cap. There was no way to tell if he'd heard, but maybe she'd gotten lucky and he hadn't. "Just let me pay and leave in peace, for heaven's sake."

"If that's what you want." Sally took the cash, counted it, and glanced up at Haley. "You need your change?"

"No, of course not." She tucked her wallet back in her jeans pocket and picked up her box. "Although I should keep the tip as compensation for all the trouble you're causing, flirting with the deputy."

Sally snorted. "Please. He's too young for me."

"Plus, you're married," Haley noted wryly.

Sally waved her off. "Emmett wouldn't care. He knows I know what side my bread's buttered on. But, girl, your toast is dry as a bone." At Haley's sharp look, Sally held up her hands, the ancient register dinging as she pushed the drawer shut with her hip. "I'm just sayin', is all."

"Have a nice day, Sally," Haley said pointedly, loudly, and then turned toward Leland. "Have a good one, Deputy."

Leland lifted his hand in a wave, throwing her a nod over his shoulder, and she felt twenty pairs of eyes on her as she waved back and headed for the doors, her cheeks warm and a tingle in her stomach that she couldn't entirely blame on her breakfast being interrupted.

The Styrofoam box squeaked loudly as she set it on the passenger's seat of her Range Rover, and her thoughts shifted to the boy at the clinic and the bite on his shoulder, the clatter she'd heard on the phone, and the restrained urgency in Karen's voice.

The chance that someone *hadn't* illegally turned a human into a werewolf on her preserve was shrinking so rapidly it wasn't even much of a question anymore. But who the heck would have done such a thing?

She thought—hoped—that none of her pack would, but if it wasn't one of hers, that meant that there were trespassers in her territory, and that came with its own set of questions. But making sure Diego was all right was her first priority, and the Range Rover kicked up gravel as she gunned it out of the parking lot.

Don't stop now. Keep reading with your copy of EDGE OF THE WOODS, by City Owl Author, Jules Kelley, available now.

And sign up for Shari Nichol's newsletter to get all the news, giveaways, excerpts, and more!

Want even more paranormal books? Try EDGE OF THE WOODS, by City Owl Author, Jules Kelley, and sign up for Shari's newsletter for more here.

There's something lurking in Pine Grove, Montana, and its bite is vicious.

Haley Fern has been the alpha of her local werewolf pack for less than a year, when their law enforcement liaison retires, and Leland Sommers, a man who knows nothing about werewolves or their world, is hired in his place.

What could be an awkward situation turns complicated when the man shows up his first day on the job with an injured teenage boy he found on the road--a boy Haley knows has just been bitten.

But discovering who bit the kid isn't as easy as it seems, especially with Leland asking questions and looking at Haley the way he does.

Can the alpha figure out who is attacking innocent people on her wildlife preserve and protect her pack? Or will the new sheriff and her growing attraction to him put her entire world in danger?

Please sign up for the City Owl Press newsletter for chances to win special subscriber-only contests and giveaways as well as receiving information on upcoming releases and special excerpts.

All reviews are **welcome** and **appreciated**. Please consider leaving one on your favorite social media and book buying sites.

For books in the world of romance and speculative fiction that embody

Innovation, Creativity, and Affordability, check out City Owl Press at www.cityowlpress.com.

ACKNOWLEDGMENTS

This book wouldn't be possible without the patience and brilliance of my editor, Heather McCorkle. Thank you for making my books better! Thank you to everyone at City Owl Press. I appreciate it so much! I want to shout out a big thank you to Mark B. for giving me his raw, honest feedback. Thank you for encouraging me to turn this one little idea about a coven of witches into a four book series. Thank you to Lara Zee. You give a good beta read. And to the readers, thank you for letting me come into your lives. Your continued love and support means the world!

Xoxo

Shari

Would you like to stay up on all the latest news? Sign up for my newsletter here.

ABOUT THE AUTHOR

Shari Nichols grew up in a small town in Connecticut where haunted houses, ghosts and Ouija boards were common place, spurring her fascination with all things paranormal. Ever since she read her first Barbara Cartland novel, her life-long dream has been to write sexy, romantic stories. When she's not writing, she's reading, going to the gym, or hanging out with family and friends.

She lives in New Jersey with her husband, two children, and her golden retriever. Shari's a member of Romance Writers of America, New Jersey Romance Writers, Liberty States Fiction Writers and Fantasy, Futuristic, and Paranormal Romance Writers. Sign up for her newsletter here.

Awards: Golden Leaf Finalist, NJ Author Best Book Finalist, The Beverley Award, HOLT Medallion Finalist, Literary Titan Silver Medal Winner.

sharinicholsauthor.com

ABOUT THE PUBLISHER

City Owl Press is a cutting edge indie publishing company, bringing the world of romance and speculative fiction to discerning readers.

Escape Your World. Get Lost in Ours!

www.cityowlpress.com

[f] facebook.com/YourCityOwlPress

[twitter] twitter.com/cityowlpress

[instagram] instagram.com/cityowlbooks

[pinterest] pinterest.com/cityowlpress